...with a splash of Kay

...with a splash of Kay

Kelly Benoit

NEW DEGREE PRESS

COPYRIGHT © 2023 KELLY BENOIT

...with a splash of Kay

ISBN

979-8-88926-944-1 *Paperback*

979-8-88926-987-8 *Ebook*

To the female authors, activists, and naysayers who
came before us, each generation stands on the former's
shoulders to shape, grow, and flourish what they ignited.
I'm grateful for your boundary-breaking ways.

To my fierce girlfriends, whose vulnerability and laughter bring me
endless joy, I've embodied the spirit of your friendship in these pages.

To my family, who shaped my experiences and
continue to encourage my journey, thank you.

To my partner, Mario, who provides unwavering
support for my ambitions, I love you.

And to younger Kelly, the dreamer who turned her bedroom wall
into a collage of magazine photos resembling the life she yearned
for, you've become the woman you always aspired to be...

... and while you've learned not everything that
glitters is gold—once in a while, it is.

LaToulle

The sunlight graced my face as I left my apartment and turned toward Greene Street. Its warmth the strongest yet this year. Spring finally arrived, and the light breeze felt nice against my thin jacket pulled out from storage—the clear bin under my full-size bed—this morning. I looked down to see the sun's rays illuminating the few pieces of lint from under my bed. I dusted them off, tucked my long, wavy auburn hair behind my ear, and put in earbuds.

With a forced air of confidence, I started my daily commute to LaToulle Relations, the PR firm I worked at. Having choked up during yesterday's team meeting, I was determined to approach work with a new attitude—unbothered. Easier said than done as the stain of embarrassment after losing my words played over and over in my head.

I focused my attention on the colorful flowers sprouting from the New York City sidewalks. I told myself that if I could just get through today, I'd brush off yesterday's stain like I did the lint on my jacket. Even better, it was Friday, and I had two parties at Lola's, the lounge and bar I used to bartend at when I first moved to the city after graduating from college.

At LaToulle, I took the elevator to the twenty-seventh floor, where our enthusiastic receptionist greeted everyone. "Good morning, Kay!" he said zealously.

"Good morn—" I tried to reply when out of nowhere, I felt a heavy pressure on my foot.

"Oh my gosh!" The receptionist shrieked when he realized our janitor ran over my foot with his cart. I looked down with regret at my orange flats. While they added a pop of color to my dark boyfriend jeans, white blouse, and beige jacket, they brought attention to my long feet.

"Geez," the janitor grunted before continuing to stroll his cart down the hall.

"Are you all right?" the receptionist asked. He stood up behind his desk to peak at my feet.

"All good, thanks." I quickly looked around, hoping no one else saw what had happened.

It had been nearly two years since I was hired as a creative associate at LaToulle, yet I still wasn't used to our all-white office overlooking uptown Manhattan. Perched in Midtown East, we kept everything inside pristine to impress our daily client list of influencers, moguls, and celebrities. Mostly all brought in from the firm's founder and CEO, Samantha LaToulle.

Samantha was a B-list corporate leader but an A-list PR woman. She founded LaToulle Relations more than three decades ago, but it looked like she'd only been alive for two of them. A self-described "Latina firecracker," Samantha donned an incredible sense of style and self daily. She exhibited her Peruvian heritage through the bright colors she often wore in the office and on the covers of every New York magazine, including the *New York Times* Business and Fashion sections—twice.

I swiped my badge on a security switch to open the double glass doors leading to our open workspace. Each LaToulle employee had an assigned ergonomic workstation equipped with a standing desk, split keyboard, and footrest. All of it white: the monitors, chairs, and marble floors, the ceiling and noise makers attached that muffled our gossip—white.

On my way to my desk, I admired the new art installation the building staff was hanging. Rotated twice a year, this newest installment displayed several of the many liquor brands we represented—Amore Tequila, Tulu Vodka, and Woosley Bourbon—with their brand names highlighted in neon. It was the only bit of color sprinkled within the office.

I hung my sweater in the nearly unidentifiable coat closet, only visible by a small white hook. No personal items were to be hung on our chairs or placed on our desks. Samantha emphasized the importance of perception. According to our employee handbook, she took this belief so far that she even prohibited foods with scent in the office. We could only eat and store odorless, packaged foods, like unsalted peanuts or dried fruit.

The firm saw too many important clients each day, coming in and out for pitch meetings, liquor samplings, and food pairings. Some of my colleagues and friends found it anal, but I didn't mind. My job was one many recent graduates only dreamed of having. Even if it hardly covered my student loan payments, I was grateful to work somewhere with so much clout.

On my desk sat a large document propped above my keyboard.

"What is this?" I asked Andre, Samantha's assistant, who has worked for her since she started the firm. He sat beside me, outside Samantha's office, and always arrived earlier than anyone else. He and his husband both worked for Samantha, his husband as her personal chef. I imagined she consumed their world more than I'd personally prefer her to consume mine.

"And good morning to you too!" Andre said elaborately. Everything about him was excessive, from his personality to the big brass rings he wore daily. I even noticed he added a new one today as he leaned in to whisper, "That's a brief from Samantha. I think she'd like you to review it before next week's pitch meeting with Henry's Gin."

I picked up what could have been a hundred-page manuscript. It wasn't unlike Samantha to throw work at us at the last minute, but why would I be part of a meeting with a potential client? To date, as a creative associate, I supported our existing clients by curating and copyediting campaign materials but never interacted with them directly.

Andre continued to whisper, "Christy quit yesterday." He was referring to one of three client leads at LaToulle, who were one level above associate in our firm's hierarchy.

I raised an eyebrow, ready to sip the tea. Without speaking, Andre knew that I knew that he knew more.

"She seemed unhappy for some time, and yesterday, she just walked out." He looked around deviously. He loved to gossip about the office, almost as much as he loved finding out about it first.

"So, do you think Samantha is considering me for the role?" I asked.

He widened his eyes to suggest, *duh.* Not wanting to push him further, I nodded.

"Okay," he continued, unable to stop himself. "Samantha asked me to download something on her laptop this morning, and I saw an email from a board member who agreed she could promote someone internally. Don't. Say. Anything."

LaToulle is a private equity backed firm, meaning Samantha had more stakeholders to answer to than just clients. She had a group of investors watching her every move to ensure she delivered results that kept everyone financially satisfied. I mimed myself zipping up my lips and turning a key before looking at my computer screen, masking my internal smile.

Though I'd sat next to Andre since I started, he was still a mystery to me. I often wondered what he did in his free time: If he ate dinners with his husband and Samantha or if they sat at home thinking about how to make her happy. Regardless, I valued how much he loved his job and adored Samantha. Even more, I could tell he liked me the most, even if his sassiness didn't always convey that.

As Samantha's assistant, Andre managed her calendar, travel, and expenses.. Though, because he'd worked at LaToulle for so long, he also understood the client work and would often help me and the other creative associate, Natasha.

Natasha often treated Andre like a doormat, which was such a pity. Not only did she miss out on his humor, but anyone savvy enough should know assistants hold all the secrets to an office. Get on their good side and they will not only squeeze you in on an executive's calendar or drop good words for you, but they may share those secrets with you too.

Fortunately, Andre could hold his own. He wasn't one to accept an attitude unless he was the one giving it.

On the other hand, I had a harder time standing up to Natasha. I was sure she believed I was her biggest hurdle to success at LaToulle, which only exasperated her need to work against me rather than with me. We both wanted to prove ourselves, but she made her prerogative known by frequently serving backhanded compliments, ignoring my emails, and remaining uninterested in getting to know me personally.

While Natasha had been at LaToulle slightly longer than me, Samantha recently began assigning me more client work, like this Henry's Gin brief. This was why, if Natasha heard what Andre saw in Samantha's inbox, it could equip her with more disdain toward me. She had been competitive ever since I started, and I had no doubt she'd try and sabotage any chance I had at getting a promotion—if she wasn't doing so already.

—

"Good morning, sunshines!"

Andre and I both peered our heads up to see Natasha walk in. Unlike the rest of my colleagues, Natasha's attire was dull and drab. Contrary to my more bohemian-meets-professional style, she only wore dry-cleaned, well-tailored button-down shirts, slacks, and glasses with a thick black frame. She typically pulled her short brown hair in a slick low ponytail. She looked expensive but not particularly fashionable, which is why it surprised me to learn she moved from Montreal's downtown district, where fashion was everywhere.

"Andre, is that a scarf I see on your chair?" she asked with her usual air of intimidation. "It is a little chilly in here today, but you should know better. Samantha will be walking in any minute, and that needs to go in the staff closet." She pointed to the closet door.

"Well, it's a good thing Samantha is already here and wasn't salty about my scarf like you, isn't it?" As a fifty-some-thing-year-old man, he wasn't afraid to clap back. I mean, who did she think she was anyway? Andre had worked here forever.

"Oh, Kay. I love those shoes on you. So nice to see you wear something flattering," Natasha smirked as she sat down at her desk, which rounded out our tripod setup.

Though I would have loved to say, *So nice if you wouldn't talk to me*, I disliked conflict more than I disliked her. So, I succumbed to, "Um, thank you."

Later that day, after uncomfortably sitting next to Natasha for most of the morning, Samantha held an impromptu brainstorming meeting with a few colleagues and us. The intention of these meetings was to spark creativity in a nonhierarchical environment. But let's face it, we were all just trying to prove who could come up with the best idea to impress her. And today, we needed to generate slogans to present to the Henry's Gin team in a couple weeks.

Like all of our brainstorms, I approached this one with silence and a lot of listening. I'd hardly gotten through the novel Samantha dropped off at my desk earlier that morning and didn't want to come across ill prepared.

—

"We should say, 'You own it,'" one of the client managers debated. We had been brainstorming slogans for about forty-five minutes.

"No. It needs to be, 'We own it,'" Samantha shot back after she, like me, sat quietly for the entirety of the meeting. But she was quiet for a different reason. Our brainstorms were Samantha's favorite. After hearing multiple opinions and debates, the firecracker within her became lit, and today was no different.

"We need Henry's customers to swallow the illusion that they are part of something bigger than themselves," Samantha continued as she got up from her seat. "Hand me that marker," she directed one of our client leads.

Samantha struck the marker against the whiteboard wall. Her elaborate ruffled sleeves bounced as she vigorously drew a myriad of symbols and words, including *we*, repeatedly on the board.

It looked like a masterpiece by the time she finished. She was radiant and struck a balance of motivation with intimidation. Yet what I found most commendable was her ability to command respect from everyone she stepped into a room with. Her reputation superseded her because Samantha's visions were always revolutionary.

In just the last few years, she was responsible for establishing Tulu's Vodka as the number one vodka across America, inadvertently making all classic vodka brands nearly obsolete, and elevated Fireflame to every bar's shot of choice, even earning it placements on several TV networks. So, when she asked for something, people delivered.

"This is what you need to use as inspiration. Wrap your heads around it and get me your best idea for Monday. Millions of people don't think about drinking gin, so let's get them thinking about it," she demanded again as she made her way toward the door.

"And Kay," she continued, pointing her index finger at me, "read the briefing I left on your desk in advance. You're joining me at the meeting with Henry's in two weeks, and I need you on top of it. I also need you to participate, unlike today."

Did I really just get called out in front of everyone? This was my downside. Samantha frequently complimented my work. I was always early with it and incredibly well-prepared. But I often lost confidence in a group setting and had trouble speaking up or contributing to team discussions.

"Okay, back to work, everyone!" With that, Samantha and her elaborate sleeves left the room. I couldn't help but wonder how long it would take me to gain that same confidence she exuded.

As the rest of the staff returned to their desks, I grabbed Natasha. "Can we talk on Monday? It would be good to go over our work for the week, with so many new projects going on." I was eager to improve our relationship, especially because I knew my assignment to Henry's could make her feel slighted.

"Um, sure, but I'm not sure what we need to talk about." *Of course.* Every time I tried with her, she used it as an excuse to make me feel small.

I pushed a little more. "Just so you and I are on the same page. Especially if I'll be in the Henry's meeting, I'd like to make sure I've got everything covered, and I know you were helping the leads bring them in."

She gave in. "Okay, sure. And good luck at that meeting. Just don't forget your voice." She added insult to the invisible injury from Samantha's comment. I chuckled at her sarcasm when I really wanted to know what her problem was.

The embarrassment from today's brainstorm meeting replaced yesterday's and lingered as I rounded out my day. That's why when five o'clock rolled around, I grabbed my jacket and eagerly left to get ready for the first of two parties I'd attend at Lola's this weekend.

No one asked me about my plans on my way out, which was fortunate, because I preferred my history as a bartender, and continued affiliation with the lounge, to remain private. Considering how insecure I was at LaToulle, I enjoyed the security of Lola's. Only a walk across the park away, no one ruffled me there.

Jungle Juice

The lights streamed in neon colors from every direction as tropical house music blasted throughout the rooftop at Lola's Lounge and Bar. I'd never seen the space as animated as it was for tonight's themed party, *Jungle House*. Acrobatic dancers swung from fake vines attached to an apparatus positioned over the crowd as an unusually warm March breeze flowed through Manhattan. Spring was approaching, which evoked excitement for the warmer seasons ahead.

Sisi, my best friend and aspiring part owner of Lola's, stood next to me. We met here years ago while bartending together before I left to build a career in public relations while she continued flourishing hers at the lounge.

Sisi was a Jersey girl who moved to the city to escape her parents. She found a string of restaurant jobs to afford her uptown rent shared with three other roommates until she found Lola's. Here, she not only made twice as much money, but she also found her footing. After only a couple of years at Lola's, she became their general manager. She now had an eye toward investing, planning to use tonight's party as another way to demonstrate she knew how to make them money.

As we looked out over the city lights, I saw another jungle. A concrete jungle no less, but it struck me with similar exotism and uncertainty. The same way living in the wild could.

"I probably overdid it with the acrobats, huh?" Sisi asked. We turned toward the venue and laughed as a dozen of them swung around.

"Not at all, Si. This is a vibe! Plus, bigger is typically better," I reassured her.

"Like these nails, right?" She showed off her long red nails dazzled with rhinestones. They matched her spray tan and wavy blonde extensions that covered two-thirds of her back, which, by the way, wasn't for the party. This is how Sisi always looked—extra, fabulous, and like *The Real Housewives* could recruit her at any time. Kind of funny, us standing side-by-side. We couldn't look more contrary to the other.

"And the DJ is everything!" I continued to compliment her party.

"He's cute too," she said, raising her eyebrows. Sisi had been trying to set me up on dates lately because it'd been about a year since I ended my last situationship. He was an investor at Lola's. Wealthy, good-looking, charming, but unavailable. I fell for him, and he fell for me, yet he still "wasn't ready."

Had I been dating since? Yes. Had it been anything substantial? No. If you're a single girl in her twenties, you don't need me to tell you why I'm cynical. After a year of bad dates, ghosters, and lackluster intimacy with the several guys who made it past a few dinners, I couldn't handle it anymore. But Sisi kept telling me, "You need a real one, Kay." Her trying again tonight came as no surprise.

"And I heard he thinks you're cute too. I'll introduce you both later," she continued before walking into the crowd.

"We'll see about that!" I shouted over the music before making my way back to the table she had reserved for us. After dodging the acrobatic dancers swinging above the crowd, I caught a glimpse of the DJ. He was tall, brown, and appeared confident as his hand rotated the vinyl record and his body rocked effortlessly to his own beats. *Hm, he is cute.*

At our table was Olivia, my friend who I also bartended with at Lola's. Living off a trust fund, Olivia only intended to work at Lola's briefly to please her parents by showing them she could get a job. But she stayed for two years because of the friends she made and the fun we had. Now, she was a freelance stylist, landing gigs here and there based on her family's connections.

As usual, Olivia looked gorgeous tonight. She wore high heels and a sparkly designer dress that snugged her thin, fair frame and complemented her blunt bob styled, brown hair. She had a defined jawline and high cheekbones, allowing her to get away with such a bold cut.

Rounding out the table were a couple of Olivia's friends from a recent Broadway show she worked on, along with her on-and-off again fling, Bryan, whom she never referred to as anything more than a friend.

"Kay, you remember Bryan, right?" she asked as he held his arm around her. I could only assume they were *on* again.

"Of course. Hey, Bryan!" Olivia's bubbly personality and good looks attracted many people to her over the years, but Bryan was the only one she had dated for longer than a few weeks.

"Bryan is also coming to my half-birthday brunch tomorrow!" I couldn't tell if she was excited because he would be there or because she loved celebrating herself. Regardless, I indulged her as she described the party, which would also be at Lola's. A relief for me because, for once, I didn't have to pay for one of her lavish celebrations, which I could hardly ever afford but was always too timid to say anything about.

"Kay! What do you want? We're getting another bottle," she asked.

"Up to you, Liv!"

"Let's do tequila! We need tequila."

I regretted not suggesting seltzers, something less intense, but quickly forgot when I remembered drinks were free for us at Lola's anyway.

I no longer drank as often as I used to, but tonight was different. The investor group was considering Sisi joining them as a part owner. She was eager to use her debut party as a way to show the other, mostly older investors that she had a handle on the operations and understood Lola's evolving clientele of successful, diverse millennials and Gen Zers.

So far, so good. The jungle theme was a hit, and a line of people—influencers, young entrepreneurs, and a unique group of the comic-con-going type who appreciated a good theme party—wrapped around the building in their provocative outfits and faux fur. It was a night not just for social media but for each other. Between the dancers, the jungle juice, and the overall atmosphere, it was clear everyone was having a good time.

Especially for me, after what felt like an eight-day workweek at my office, this party couldn't have come at a better time. Between Samantha's demands and my mostly empty dating life, I needed this escape, even if I'd regret the hangover in the morning. Even though so many good-looking, wealthy people surrounded me, I felt confident here. I'd worked at Lola's for so many years it now felt like a second home. Contrary to how I felt at LaToulle.

Amid intoxicated guests, I spotted Sisi moving from one side of the floor to the other. While everyone else was enjoying the evening, she couldn't until it was over. I gazed proudly from afar, knowing how hard she'd worked on this. That was until I saw her moving toward me.

"Kay, I need you to help me figure out the cords at the DJ booth. People keep stepping on them, and I don't want him to lose power!"

"Yeah, okay, Si. He's cute, but I'm not going over there." I waved my hand to shrug off her attempt at a meet cute.

"No, Kay, I—"

"Sisi, do you remember Bryan?" Olivia shouted over our table of tequila bottles and ice buckets. Annoyed, Sisi shifted her gaze at Olivia, shooting her a look that would have scared anyone. She was the only person I knew who could intimidate Olivia like that.

"Kay. Please!" she asked me again. Clearly, she did need help, so I made my way to the booth.

I had no idea what the issue was, but my reputation as the *fixer* from when I worked at Lola's stayed with me. Whenever the credit card machine would go down or the music system stopped working, everyone relied on me as the IT guru.

I wiggled through the dense crowd and the few clusters of groupies blocking the booth to reach a pile of black wires. Trying to navigate them became impossible because those same groupies were bumping into my back. So, I slid myself under the table and turned my iPhone flashlight on, which worsened the problem as an endless flood of wires became visible. I had no idea how to make sense of it all.

"What are you doing down there?" a deep voice asked as light from the rooftop shined on me. Assuming it was the

DJ, I froze. I realized my dress had risen above my panties at this point, and he could probably see it.

"Hello?" the voice asked again. Embarrassed, I rotated my head slowly over my shoulder to see I was right. It was the DJ. Heat flashed over my face as he most likely could see up my dress.

"Um, one minute!" I turned my attention back to the floor, glossing my hands over the wires instead of pulling down my dress. The heat on my face only grew hotter as I stretched my arms out. I tried to appear like I knew what I was doing while my dress slid up my backside even more.

"If I didn't know any better, I'd think you were going to end my set," he said, still hovering above me. That was when I finally spotted a wire jutting out on the dance floor. Nearly unplugged, I pulled it back and secured it around another wire so it wouldn't slip out again.

"Quite the opposite," I said. I peered my head over my shoulder again, this time catching him move his gaze from my butt to my face before we locked eyes. He knew that I knew that he just checked me out.

"Huh?" he asked.

I got up from under the booth to fix my hair and adjust myself. When I stood next to him, he was about six inches taller and even more handsome up close. I cocked my gaze slightly up to meet his.

"You asked if I was trying to cut you off. Quite the opposite," I repeated, hoping the heat from my face had dissolved.

"What's your name?" he asked deadpan.

I had an immediate attraction to his intensity. Or maybe it was the tequila. "I'm Kay."

"What are you doing here?"

"Aside from saving your set?" I asked sarcastically, my liquor courage kicking in.

He stepped back to spin his vinyl again. He held up his left index finger to signal, *Hold on a moment,* but I felt disheveled and silly standing there for a few awkward seconds that seemed like minutes.

What am I waiting for? I headed back to my table.

"Hey, where are you going?" He grabbed my hand.

"I was just here to save my best friend's night. She's hosting the party." Though I really wanted to say, *I hardly know you, let go.*

"Oh, so you're the friend I need to meet?"

"Great set." I gently released his hand and walked away. As cute as he was, any city girl knows not to mess with a DJ. If you think the guys you meet online can be players, just try a DJ.

But as I walked back to the table, my attraction for him made me want more. I turned back and saw he was looking at me intently. I felt the intensity from his eyes down my back and below my dress again. Feeling nude while fully clothed, I almost hoped he would stop me for the second time, like I was more desirable than the swarm of women around him. But he didn't.

"Where did you go?" Olivia asked. As always, she was oblivious to anyone but herself.

"Sisi needed help by the DJ booth, remember?"

"Oh yeah! He's a snack." As if I needed one more person to tell me that.

"Yes, and a DJ," I said, insinuating he was not worth it.

"Well, he's looking over here." As exciting as it was to maybe be wanted, I'd hope to know better by now that if I were going to meet someone serious, I'd be sure they didn't come with a pack of groupies.

"They always want what they can't have, huh?" Olivia asked.

"Is that why you don't let Bryan have you?" I asked—my liquor courage at its peak.

"We're just hooking up, Kay. It's not that serious. Plus, he's taking care of the liquor at my party tomorrow. Seems like a fair trade."

"Hm, I guess so." I clinked my glass with hers. Despite that their relationship was exhausting and kind of toxic, I let it go and enjoyed the rest of the night dancing with Olivia and her friends.

A couple of hours and heel blisters later, I was ready to leave. "Liv, I'm headed out of here! It's past my bedtime. I'll see you tomorrow for your party."

"It's only two o'clock in the morning!" she said. "But you're right, without cocaine, I'm not staying much longer either."

After a few air kisses across the table and a quick congratulations to Sisi, I left. I needed to work on the Henry's brief before Monday, and I didn't need a bad hangover, or a desirable DJ, to prevent that.

Bubbly

"Glad you're finally here." Olivia greeted me with a sassy undertone when I arrived at Lola's the next day for her half-birthday party.

"Doesn't the party start at two?" I asked. It was only one forty-five.

"Early is on time, and I needed you here early, early." *Aggressive for someone in a sparkly, multicolor flapper dress and high heels.* Nonetheless, her comment induced guilt, and I tried defending myself.

"I just rushed here! I was reading a packet for work all morning, and I'm sor—" But before I could finish, she interrupted.

"Uh, whatever. Just come see how everything looks." She yanked me toward the lounge area where Sisi was setting up drinks and decorations. She wore a strapless black bralette, high wasted black leggings, and Gucci loafers.

"Hey, Si, need help with anything?" I asked.

"Hey! Nah, all set, girl. Thanks!" Sisi swiped her long extensions over her bare shoulder.

Olivia not-so-quietly whispered to me, "She put the party down here because she 'doesn't have time' to turn over the main floor before the next party coming tonight." She used air quotes and rolled her eyes.

"Because they actually paid me for the space, unlike you!" Sisi yelled as she placed champagne bottles on ice. "Geez, you act like I can't hear you. You're lucky I've done any of this. Do you realize what my schedule is like this week?"

"Clearly too busy to care about a theme!" Olivia said, pointing out Sisi's disregard for the 1920s theme we were supposed to dress for.

"Yeah, exactly. Because one of us actually works," Sisi snickered. They'd been on edge with each other for some time, but things recently escalated because Sisi was under more stress while working toward her own promotion. Her bullshit radar was at an all-time high, even for her.

Fortunately, Olivia just ignored her. It was amazing her ability to disregard any backlash her insensitive comments received. Instead, she brought me to the corner of the room and turned me around to look at the entirety of the space.

Lola's lounge was in its basement and darker than the main floor and rooftop. Down here, there were no windows, just an open room with a big wooden, rectangular table centered in the middle. The chairs were large with red velvet fabric, each rumored to cost a thousand dollars. Gold-trimmed portraits of burlesque costume wear hung along the walls.

Apparently, it was a speakeasy space in the 1920s—which you'd think would go perfectly with the theme—but Olivia was still underwhelmed and likely would have booked another restaurant had she known her party would be in the lounge. She had no problem splurging her family's money on herself.

"What do you think?" Olivia asked me. The decorations were lackluster, with a few sparkled balloons and one flimsy sign drooped along the wall in gold that read, "LET'S PARTY."

A few buckets of free champagne bottles Sisi had collected over the prior months sat on ice next to cheese and crackers. It was a total mismatch with the dark furniture and red velvet chairs.

"Looks great!" I fibbed.

"No, it doesn't. This looks ridiculous," Olivia shot back.

"We can pump the music and keep the champagne running. Everyone will be fine," Sisi chimed in from across the room again.

"Hopefully, they don't see what kind of champagne this is." Olivia held up a bottle. "I mean, have you ever heard of this before?" I did not want to get involved. Besides, Bryan would bring some of the alcohol brands he represented anyway.

"Forget about it, Liv, and happy half-birthday! Here's a half-gift for you." I handed Olivia a small gift box as a gesture that I was invested in what I actually believed was an over-the-top celebration. It was a client sample I took from my office a couple of weeks back. A beautiful marble-cased wine set, it came with a brass bottle opener, two bulbous wine glasses, and a decanter. I imagined she'd use it in her spacious, granite kitchen where she frequently entertained guests.

"Oh geez, you shouldn't have," Olivia said as she opened the gift. I stood there silent and confused. "Sisi, can you put this in the office or something?" Olivia grimaced, appearing as enthused about the gift as she was about the lounge space.

"Sure, but maybe you should tell Kay, 'Thank you,' first," Sisi said.

"Why? I assume you got this from your office. Right, Kay? Not to mention, I don't drink wine." I was mortified. She was right. I shouldn't have gotten her anything. It was only her half-birthday. On top of it, I felt ashamed she outed me for taking it from my office.

"You're an unappreciative bitch, Olivia," Sisi said.

"The unappreciative birthday bitch! Come, let's grab drinks before everyone gets here!" Again, Olivia effortlessly blew off other's disregard for her behavior. I just grinned and bared it.

Over the next hour, about thirty of Olivia's friends from college and the recent production she worked on arrived. They were a mix of young girls in designer clothes and middle-aged actors with a unique sense of style. It was an odd crowd. One I didn't quite identify with. I sipped mostly water, aside from her friend's poor attempt at a champagne tasting and game of, "Who knows Olivia best?"

Throughout, I tried interacting with her friends but found most of our conversations fell flat. When I finally saw Sisi— who was running around the restaurant to prepare for the night ahead—I grabbed her.

"Please don't leave me here alone with these people again," I begged.

"I know! They're terrible. But Romano isn't here or answering his phone." She was referring to Lola's assistant manager, who'd only started about a month ago, though Sisi often complained about his laziness.

"Well, he's late sometimes, right? I'm sure he'll show up."

"Yeah, I hope so. Not only do I have several parties tonight, but the leak in the upstairs bathroom is running down the wall and onto the lounge floor." I looked where Sisi pointed and saw a few floorboards raised from the water. "All I need is for one of these losers to trip and sue us." She glared at Olivia's friends in a group posing with the champagne bottles.

"Ah, Milo, you're here!" Sisi walked toward the door and greeted a guy who looked our age. He wore dark jeans and thick brown construction boots, both covered in paint smudges. His broad shoulders and chiseled arms poked through his white shirt. Sisi showed him the affected floor-boards before Olivia came over to us, visibly annoyed.

"What is that guy doing down here?" she asked Sisi.

"That's my handyman, and he's here to fix everything the last manager neglected."

"Well, he shouldn't be here *now*, during *my* party."

"Oh, please. You're not that special." Sisi disregarded her and left the room. Once again, I was left to fend for myself.

"So, Kay. What was up with you and the DJ last night? He was cayyyute!" Olivia asked.

"Nothing! Si wanted to make it a thing, but it wasn't."

"That's too bad. You need to get some, girl. It's been a while."

"Hm, maybe," I trailed off. "What about you and Bryan? He's not here today?" If she could ask me about my dating life, I should have permission to ask about hers.

"Um, he had another thing today. It's fine. I'm not trying to be something with him anyway." She hadn't convinced me of her honesty.

"Really? You two seemed to hit it off last night." I was nervous she'd think I was prying, but to my surprise, Olivia divulged me.

"We had a great time! We went to my friend's after-party. You know, the tall guy with highlighted hair at our table. He was the director of my last show. Anyway, we get there, and Kay, there is cocaine everywhere. Oh, my goodness, we got so high, and then Bryan took me to the side balcony of the building. We had sex on it overlooking the city." As unhinged as Olivia was, at least her stories were entertaining.

"So fun! It's too bad he couldn't make it today."

"Why? I told you I don't want to be with him." I finally hit a nerve. "Whatever, I'm going to get more of this crappy champagne and find out where our food is. I'm starving."

"Oh, that's right! I'll check on it. You go enjoy yourself." I motioned for her to return to her party. Luckily, she accepted my offer.

In the kitchen, I peeked at what looked like leftovers. The spread included a sad looking fruit tray—you know, mostly melon and cantaloupe—one large Caesar salad, a barrage of popcorn chicken, three platters of french fries, and a giant soup bowl. The soup certainly consisted of leftover beef that likely would be thrown out in a day or two if not used up. As a former restaurant worker, the evidence was clear—Sisi told the kitchen to concoct what was cheap or would spoil. I laughed to myself at the thought of it.

Seeing as the food was ready for the party, I dashed to the unisex bathroom in an attempt to avoid playing soundboard for Olivia's complaints when she saw what the chef cooked up.

"Oh my god, I'm so sorry!" I exclaimed after walking in on the handyman in the bathroom. Thankfully, he was only washing his hands—the best kind of walk-in.

"All good! You're about a few seconds too late from this being a lot more awkward." He had a Spanish-speaking accent and one dimple that appeared when he spoke.

"Okay, great, because I'm really just trying to duck out from that party."

"Why is that?" he asked.

"Oh, no reason. I just have work to do later and can't drink too much." As cute as he was, I didn't want to flirt with the handyman in a bathroom.

"Ah, got it. Well, good luck down there!" He waved and passed by me in the doorway.

"Thanks!" I locked myself in the bathroom and took a few minutes before returning to the lounge. I must have missed Olivia's reaction to the food because everyone was seemingly content as they ate the leftovers. I took a seat at the table between an empty chair on my right and a girl on my left who looked familiar.

"Hey, you went to school with Olivia, right?" I asked her. "I'm Kay, her friend from our days working at Lola's."

"Yeah, we did. How's the chicken?"

"I haven't tried it yet, but it seems good," I said.

"I'm so weird with chicken." She turned to another girl on her left. "Did you try the chicken?" The girl shook her head no. "Uh, I don't know. I'm just so picky with my chicken." She pushed her plate away and got up from the table. At the same time, someone sat in the chair next to me, hitting my armrest as they did.

It was the handyman. His paint-stained boot maneuvered over the seat cushion before he sat down and pulled his chair between his legs and toward the table.

"Mind if I sit here?"

"What if I did? Would you get up and leave?" I asked sarcastically.

"Yeah, I probably would," he said, seemingly dismissing my joke.

"I'm Kay, by the way."

"I'm starving, but I also go by Milo." His attempt at a joke was corny at best. But he also had curly, short brown hair, broad shoulders, and an innocently handsome face that made up for it.

"Hi, Milo. Nice to *officially* meet you. Are you sure you want to stay and eat with us?"

"Considering it's a free meal and I'm hungry, this seems like a good deal to me. What's so bad about you all anyway?"

"Well, try not to group me in with everyone. I just know the birthday girl. But okay. Look, that girl over there." I pointed to the "weird with chicken" girl. "She is freaking out about poultry."

"What does that even mean?" he asked.

"Exactly."

Milo cut his chicken breast into a hefty-sized piece, tilted his head, and bit it off his fork. "Tastes pretty damn good."

"I think you're just hungry." I withheld my distaste for his lack of manners. "So, how did you start working at Lola's?" I asked as he continued to chew his food.

"I stopped by a few weeks ago with friends and realized the place needed a lot of work. I'm in grad school at Columbia, but I'm paying down my loans with these side jobs." I admired his openness. "So, I asked Sisi if she needed someone to fix up the place. Turns out she did, and now I'm here. Eating chicken with you. At a birthday party you don't want to be at." *Lacks etiquette but funny.*

"Let me guess. You're in school for an MBA?"

"No, no. Architecture. You couldn't tell?"

"How would I be able to tell that?"

"I'm not the MBA type, a little too grungy for that." I laughed at his humility.

"So, I guess you find the food is better at Lola's than the floorboards?"

"Huh?"

"Nevermind, bad joke," I said, embarrassed of my attempted humor.

He took another bite of chicken. "Be right back. I'm gonna go see what that soup is about."

When he got up, Olivia sat down. "Why is that guy here? I didn't invite the plumber."

"He's not a plumber!" *Not that it would matter if he were.*

"Well, whatever. Where's Sisi?"

"I think she's in the office doing some work." I didn't want Olivia to know Sisi was avoiding the party.

"Well, if you see her, tell her to skip the dessert. This whole thing is an embarrassment, and my friend ordered a Milk Bar cake for delivery to my apartment, so we're out of here. I'd rather be on my rooftop than in this dungeon."

"Okay, sure. I'll let her know." I figured it'd be best if Olivia didn't say bye to Sisi at this point.

"Thanks. Are you coming?" Olivia asked me.

"I can't, Liv. I have too much work to do." I was only half-lying. While I did, in fact, have work to do, I certainly wasn't planning to do any more of it tonight. The reality was I didn't want to get suckered into a late night of drinking and spending money. Knowing Olivia, she'd want to get bottle service at some fancy club.

"You're always working. You need to live more." She then got up to wrangle her friends.

"Have fun!" I optimistically said as she walked away.

To avoid goodbyes, I left the room to find Sisi. Lola's new assistant manager, Romano, still hadn't shown up, and she needed me to pick up some drapes to cover the construction on the main floor. To avoid Olivia's lingering friends who were calling their rideshares and likely would ask me to join in with them, I snuck out the side door.

As I neared the subway station, I saw my train approaching and rushed to the platform. Simultaneously, my phone vibrated. After jumping into the train, panting and self-conscious from my desperate run to make it on time—I mean, who leaves a decadent brunch to rush to a train to avoid paying a few extra bucks for a taxi?—I checked my phone.

Unknown number: On the off chance you don't have a party to entertain tonight, I'd like to see you

Who the hell was this? Oh, that's right. It must be the DJ. Uh, Sisi!

Añejo and Lemon

After getting caught in a flash mob of rollerbladers in wigs, blasting disco music throughout midtown, I made it back to Lola's. I dropped off the drapes with Sisi and praised her for last night's wildly successful jungle party since I didn't have time to earlier.

"Yeah, thanks. It would've been more enjoyable if I hadn't had Olivia's party to worry about." In typical Sisi fashion, she didn't accept praise very well and changed the subject. "What the hell is her problem anyway?" she continued while making me a tequila añejo and lemon cocktail—the best combination.

"Who, Olivia?" I asked.

"Yes, Olivia! She needs a vibe check. I just threw her that stupid birthday party, and she didn't even thank me. Ever since she started seeing Bryan again, she's been totally obnoxious and more self-centered than usual. I mean, her comment about your gift—who does that?"

"I know, I know." Sisi as she handed me my drink. Her long, red nails contrasted sharply against the translucent white glass. "Ooh, my favorite. Thank you!"

"Honestly, I don't even want her here anymore," she went on.

"So you notice it too?" I asked, thinking about how she gift shamed me.

"Notice? Kay, she is so rude to you. And there's no talking things out with her. That's why I'm just gonna do it. I'm banning her from Lola's."

I lifted my eyebrows in shock. "Woah, how are you going to do that?" I couldn't imagine being so direct with a friend. I worried for Sisi just thinking about it.

"Easy." Sisi shrugged. "I just will. I'll be fine, and so will she. She needs to understand I work too hard and that my time is valuable. I can't just throw her half-birthday parties or book tables whenever she wants. I'd much rather use that time to touch up my nails or get my lips filled." I laughed at her unintended quip. "I'll give her the shine she wants for her half-birthday today, but I'm telling her off this week." I did not want to be in the middle of these two, but she had a point.

Sisi started pacing behind the bar. "What are you looking for?" I asked.

"I don't know what I'm looking for. I'm just stressed. Romano officially quit. He just texted me."

"No way! Officially, officially?"

"Yeah! Him *and* the new bartender. She got a gig as a dancer downtown somewhere and took Romano with her. Guess they think they're better suited elsewhere. Good luck to 'em!" I hadn't met Romano, but Sisi often complained he was snarky. I tried to reassure her it was probably for the best, but she continued to vent.

"He told me he didn't care for my tone. What does that even mean? I didn't care for his lazy butt, which is actually in better shape than mine, but I didn't say anything!" We both laughed, this time at her intended quip.

"Sooo, by the way," I said slowly, leaning over the bar so no one else could hear me. "That DJ from last night texted me." I held my breath, waiting for what I assumed would be an over-the-top response. But I was met with silence as Sisi organized liquor bottles behind the bar. "Si, did you hear me?"

"What? The DJ? That's cool. I told you he's cute," she said.

"Mm, yeah. So, how'd he get my number, huh?" She ignored me again. "Si! You know I'm not going to date a DJ! I'm sure he has a ton of girls, better looking than me, waiting for him." She knew I was ready for a real relationship but had a hard stop on anyone who hinted *player*.

Since dating one of Lola's investors last year, I'd only experienced ghosting, lying, or fake romanticism from guys who were always a swipe away from the next best thing. New York men are a different breed, so I promised myself I'd stop falling too quickly and be privier to any red flags immediately, like "DJ" and the groupies that probably came with him.

"I didn't give him your number! I just said he was cute."

"If you didn't, then who did?"

"Kay, he's Bryan's friend. If you don't wanna talk to him, then just don't answer. I have too much going on here to think about that right now."

Ugh, Bryan. "I guess I don't have to respond," I said. Sisi was still pacing. "Hey, you'll find a new manager soon. Don't plenty of people want to work here?"

"You'd think that! But it's so difficult, Kay. I have to find someone and get them up to speed in a day. I'm way too busy to train somebody. I'm at the point where it's easier to stay here all the time and do it myself."

"Why not promote one of the bartenders?" I suggested.

"Please. None of them want to trade in tips for stress. I just wish I knew someone who already understood what to do." What was meant to be *my* vent session turned into Sisi's. We paused. Then, it seemed a lightbulb went off in her mind.

"Ah! I have a great idea!" She turned toward me in a swift motion, nearly getting her long hair in my drink. "*You* can help me!"

Huh?

"Please, Kay," she continued, her voice transitioning from enthusiastic to eager. "You're one of the only people I know who I wouldn't need to babysit. And it would only be after work. Or just weekends! A few hours at a time, max. I promise. At least until I find someone new to train. And you can take a bartending shift for extra cash too!"

I took a sip of my drink.

Sisi continued, "I have to prove myself to these investors. They've never had a former employee work alongside them, and I need to show them I got this. You were always so great here. And, of course, I'll pay you." Her plea was tempting. "You're here all the time anyway! Might as well make some money, right?"

Working for Samantha was prestigious, but the pay didn't reflect that. Unlike my coworkers without student debt and whose parents likely supplemented their rent, I was strapped for cash. When I worked at Lola's, I could make up to eight hundred dollars a night.

"You're right. I am here enough anyway…" my voice trailed off. She could tell I was agreeing.

"It would be a huge, *huge* help!"

"Okay, I will. *But*! I have a few requests."

"Shoot."

"I can't clock in until five-thirty, and I may be a few minutes late some days. And unless you *really* need me, I shouldn't work past eleven. I can't afford not to look snatched at the office," I joked and tossed my hair over the back of my shoulder. *Why couldn't I be this confident at LaToulle?*

"Deal!" Sisi said with relief. "How about you work Mondays? It's slower, we close early, and you can bartend and manage. I'll pay you, and you can keep your tips. "

"Sure, just not past eleven," I jokingly reminded her.

"No problem. But I still need your help tonight! Can you put those drapes in the room upstairs and check the wiring to the speakers? Your drink's on me."

"It always is!" I swiped the drapes off the bar top.

Sisi grinned until she caught the eye of a busboy carrying unpolished glasses to the dining area. "Those aren't polished!" she shouted to him. "Ugh, you see what I mean? No time!" She shrugged her shoulders and chased him into the kitchen.

I didn't know when she'd find another manager, but I figured it wouldn't be too long. Plus, my real concern wasn't whether I could handle two jobs, I had the energy for both, but whether working at a restaurant would interfere with my potential promotion at LaToulle. Samantha put such an emphasis on *image* that the thought of seeking her approval to work at Lola's put me on edge. Along with the thought of my snobby colleagues judging me or assuming I'd slack in the office as a result. *Probably best I keep this to myself.*

After I hung the drapes over the damaged wall, the evening crowd poured in. I wasn't in the mood for another party, so I decided Netflix and takeout at home were the way to go until I got another text.

DJ: Hello, is this Kay?

Thinking about my ensuing evening, maybe flirting with him was better than isolation after all. Begrudgingly, I responded.

Martini

A few minutes later, the DJ and I were in a full-blown text exchange. I learned his name is Adam, and he's spontaneous.

Adam: Let's meet for a drink?

Feeling slightly buzzed from my cocktail at Lola's and engaged in his messages, I said yes.

Kay: Where?

Adam: Where are you?

Kay: East Village

I lied. I didn't want him to know I was in Midtown on a Saturday.

Adam: I'll be there in twenty. Pick a spot.

Kay: Okay, will let you know. And let's make it thirty.

I was still wearing my fringe dress from Olivia's 1920s-themed party. A bit over the top for a first date at a bar, but I was nowhere near home to change.

Despite my less than ideal condition, I reminded myself that even when I did dress my best for a first date, it typically resulted in nothing more than a nonmutual reciprocity of feelings anyhow. Either I liked him and he never asked me out again, or he liked me and I wasn't into it.

On my way downtown, I stopped by a makeup store in hopes of uplifting my look. Pretending I wanted to buy something, I touched up my eyeliner, mascara, and foundation. I even sprayed a little perfume. I was sure the staff saw what I was doing and judged me. I made my best attempt to appear remorseful in hopes our unspoken exchange evened itself out.

—

Bars full of people and some with lines out the door saturated the East Village. "Teeny boppers," as Sisi called college-aged drinkers, occupied the sidewalks illuminated by storefront windows and the city lights. It was still raining, but that didn't prevent anyone from living their best night out.

After a couple of blocks and some texts from Adam, who was also running into bar line after bar line, I spotted a mostly empty, intimate Italian restaurant. The waitstaff stood idle after the dinner crowd had already emptied out.

"Are you all open?" I asked the host.

"For another hour," he replied, less than thrilled his shift wasn't over yet.

Tired of searching for the ideal place, I grabbed a seat at their small bar. I thought I'd have time to smooth my frizzy hair and wipe my dripping eyeliner, but then Adam walked in, his tall frame and good looks as striking tonight as they were yesterday.

"I thought I saw you come in here," he said, startling me. He wore fitted jeans with an expensive looking dark blue sweater. At just over six feet, he had soft brown eyes and an air of confidence—maybe arrogance. He seemed born with. It all made him intriguing and desirable. It all made me tense and unsure I was in his league.

"So, is this your scene?" Adam asked as he casually took the bar stool next to me and slid it between his legs. He squared his body toward mine, his legs remaining open.

Before I could answer, the bartender approached. "We're done with food service. You two just want drinks?"

"Hey man, yeah, that'd be great. Can I get a Henry's martini straight up?" Adam ordered.

"I'll take a pinot noir," I added before turning to Adam. "So, you like Henry's? Always drink gin?" *Ironic choice.*

"No, actually, not usually," Adam said. "It really depends on my mood." I tried to ignite more of a conversation, but he wasn't giving me much to work with. *Was it my outfit or the restaurant choice after all?*

The bartender came back with my red wine and a silver shaker full of Henry's gin. He added ice and vermouth before vigorously shaking and pouring it into a martini glass. His white button-down and maroon tie added to the sophistication of his performance. I made a mental note for the Henry's pitch next week.

"Do you want to start a tab?" The bow-tied bartender asked.

"Yup, here." Adam handed over his credit card without hesitation. He turned toward me with his martini in hand. "So, what's your story?"

"Well, you waste no time," I replied. "What do you want to know?"

"When was your last relationship?"

"You're really not one for small talk."

"Nope." Adam wasn't overtly playful but came across genuinely curious. As composed as I wanted to be in our conversation, this moment brought me back to when I was under the DJ booth, exposed, and underneath his eye.

"Oh, about a year ago," I said, referencing Noah, the Lola's investor. "I was in over my head... and, well, he was practical," I trailed off, unsure whether I was accurately describing our situationship or if I wanted to share more. Adam was quiet, anticipating what I'd say next. Not wanting to let him down, I indulged further. "Well, we were both pursuing our careers, meeting new people, and I don't think he was ready to commit."

"And you were?" Adam asked.

"I don't know. I guess so." I shrugged and sipped my pinot noir.

Adam gave me a look like, *And...?* Nimbly, I continued to blab. I explained why I moved to New York and about my passion for sales, media, and vibrant cities. In return, he opened up a bit. I learned he was in his early thirties and recently quit his job to pursue his budding DJ career. As he shared more, I became spellbound by his charisma. The kind that comes with a sure sense of self.

When he asked about my job, I found it hard to be honest. How could I tell him that, up until a couple of years ago, I spent my nights passing out whiskey shots at a night lounge? That I could hardly afford my apartment if it weren't for saving cash tips? I wanted him to think of me as his equal. No, actually, unattainable. So, I kept it high level and only spoke to the things I thought he'd be impressed by, like my potential account with Henry's.

"Henry's, huh? Does that mean I should have let you buy my drink?"

"Not just yet!" I pointed my finger. "I'll let you know after my meeting next week."

"Guess that means I'll see you again." I blushed and took another sip of my wine, hoping he wouldn't notice. Then, Adam pulled something from his pocket.

"What's that?"

"They're some new gummies I got. Low strain but really nice. You want one?"

"Are you dealing me drugs on our first date?" I joked.

"Oh, so this is a date?" He gave me a side-eye and popped one in his mouth. I then stuck my hand out to accept one of his foreign treats.

"It's potent," he warned. I must have looked alarmed because he assured me, "It's just a small edible and will give you a nice buzz." *Oh great, he probably thinks I'm uptight.*

"I've had cocaine and tried ecstasy a few times in college." I attempted to sound like a professional drug enthusiast. Instead, I almost certainly sounded like a teeny bopper. He laughed, hopefully not at me. *Geez, Kay, stop trying so hard.*

"Let's go somewhere else," Adam suggested. He signed the check, and we left. It stopped raining, but the temperature dropped. Not enough to need a warm jacket, but enough that a warm embrace would be comforting.

"Come, let's go this way." Adam walked me a couple of blocks to a stairwell that led to a small bar. "I know them here. Let's see if we can get a seat." Sure enough, when we walked in, a couple got up from the far end of the bar, leaving us with two seats.

"Hey, you!" A female bartender flirtatiously greeted Adam, exposing her cleavage when she bent over the bar to wipe the countertop.

"Heyyy, how are you, Jill?" She and Adam shared pleas-antries I couldn't follow. I just noticed how big her boobs were. *Shit, I'm high.*

"What?" Adam asked me.

Did I just say that out loud?

"What do you want to drink?" Jill followed up.

"Oh, um... hm, a pinot noir."

"And for you?" She asked Adam, tilting her head down but lifting her eyes up. I was sure they'd slept together before.

"Henry's martini."

"Another martini?" I questioned.

"Only because I'm having fun."

I wondered if he'd DJ'd at this bar before and if that's how he knew the bartender. But I didn't ask. Even in my high, it was obvious how little he felt the need to engage with dead-end questions.

My giving up initiating conversation surprisingly led Adam to be his most talkative yet. He told me about his music, how DJing introduces him to interesting people, and that he never wanted a boss again. I was finally getting to know him when my gummy kicked in. *Really* kicked in. I could no longer follow his sentences. With every word he spoke, I only noticed his lips moving in slow motion as his head shifted from side to side.

"I think I'm too high for this," I blurted.

"Oh yeah? How do you feel?"

"Um, good but, like, high. Really high." The bartender came back to ask if we wanted food, but all I could focus on was my head, which felt like it was spinning and melting at the same time. "I think that gummy was more potent than I expected."

"The way you took it, I thought you did them often. Probably should have started with a half there." He put his hand on my shoulder. "Is Kay okay?"

"I think I need to leave." As much as I wanted to stay, I couldn't keep my head up without struggling.

"Yeah, of course. No problem," he said before paying the tab. *At least I didn't have to worry about the bill.* "Let's get out of here so I can get you a cab." As we waited outside, Adam rubbed my upper arm. "Will you be all right getting home?"

"Yeah, I'm okay. Already feeling better," I lied. I didn't want him to think I wasn't okay. I was embarrassed by my vulnerability but thankful he wasn't someone who would take advantage of me.

A light rain picked up again as we waited for my driver. Only a drizzle, each raindrop felt heavy and cold as it hit my skin, and the sensations intensified by my high. Adam noticed. He swung his arm around my back to pull me closer to him. All night I questioned if he felt an attraction to me. Now I knew. I felt safe in his arms, the rain slowly dripping on us.

"Your car will be here any second." Adam leaned out from our embrace to look down into my eyes. He tapped my lips with his before pulling away to assess my reaction. I smiled, welcoming him to kiss me again. And he did, slowly, the sensation only intensified by my high.

I pulled away when I saw my vehicle pull up.

"I think that's your ride," he whispered softly. He turned his head toward the street, his arms still wrapped around me.

I kissed him again. "Thank you," I mustered after his lips left mine.

On my way home, the lights flickered through my cab's windows, and the rain clinked heavily on its rooftop. I wasn't sure what to make of the evening or of Adam, but it didn't stop me from replaying our kiss over and over until I fell asleep.

Rosé

—

The sound of sirens woke me up, my eyes heavy as I peered them open. I was surprised to be in my own bed, my sheets scattered like I fought myself in the night. I lay there trying to recall how I got here.

A shame hangover hit as I replayed some of my awkward conversation and inability to handle an edible. I contemplated the extent I embarrassed myself, with someone out of my league no less. I shook my head in an attempt to erase the memories.

It was eleven in the morning, way past my weekday wake-up time. *How could I have slept so long?* Lazily, I walked to the kitchen and saw I hadn't set up my coffee machine on delay brew like usual. I wasn't sure I brushed my teeth either.

I leaned against my counter, waiting for the hot coffee to finish brewing. Sunlight beamed on my arm. Its rays stretched across my apartment, warming the room. A breeze flowed through my cracked window, reminding me of when I first moved here.

I found this space after they hired me at LaToulle. At the time, I wanted to move from a two-bedroom split apartment to my own studio, even if it cost more and I made less in my LaToulle paycheck than cash tips from Lola's. But searching for an apartment in New York was grueling, with new listings typically lasting a week. More deflating, any decent listing was almost always out of my price range.

After viewing a dozen vacant spaces and meeting just as many sketchy realtors, I stumbled on my studio. It was the only one with a closet, had enough space to walk more than six steps in one direction, and, importantly, had sunlight. Birds chirped outside the bathroom window, similar to today.

Although my new rent ate up half my monthly income, I bet on my career in public relations that it'd lead me down a lucrative road over time. Hopefully, it'll even make me more money than bartending one day.

Ha. I laughed at the irony of it all. That I took my apartment as motivation to climb the corporate ladder, only to be back at Lola's anyway.

After coffee, I underwent my morning routine—washed my face, made my bed, and applied basic makeup—all while trying to push out the thoughts from the night before. I couldn't imagine Adam would want to see me again, and I didn't want to care more than I already did.

I took the rest of the day for myself, visiting a museum and binge-watching familiar TV shows. Just as I rid myself of the guilt from last night, I received a text—Adam, after all. I hesitated to open it out of the fear his message would confirm I was, in fact, an embarrassment. I toyed for a few seconds, which felt like minutes, until I gave in.

> **Adam:** I had a great time with you and want to see you again. Are you free this week?

Seriously? I was shocked but undeniably elated. As strange as our night was, I liked his spontaneity and charm, and it was also alluring that someone like him would be interested in someone like me. I think I'm into a DJ. *Damn it.*

Unpolished

Friday felt like a distant memory when I walked into LaToulle on Monday. It always baffled me how we could spend so much time at work, yet none of us knew much about one another outside of it. It's as if we all emerged from our personal world to enter our work world as toned-down, more professional versions of ourselves.

"Good morning! How was your weekend?" Our receptionist broke my thought when he greeted me overenthusiastically on the twenty-seventh floor. I didn't want to engage in small talk but felt compelled to be polite.

"Great, got to see the new exhibit at the Whitney. How was yours?" I only disclosed the tamest, most office-appropriate part of my weekend.

"Nice! Mine was great too. Really enjoying the warmer weather." *The weather? How typical.*

After several cups of coffee and a cold shower yesterday, I reviewed the brief and practiced my pitch countless times. I was confident about the content but nervous about how Samantha would perceive me.

At our desks, Andre was with a woman my age, brunette and tan. She wore a flashy floral skirt and a white ruffled top.

Her chunky gold bangles and oversized earrings dangled from her wrists and ears. She was beautiful, thin, and sitting in my chair. As I approached my desk, she gave Andre a courteous half-hug.

"Thanks, Andre! You're the best!" She smiled before bouncing off to Samantha's office.

"Who was that?" I asked.

"That's Samantha's daughter, Karole. She's taking the semester off from school because her social media presence is *thriving*, as she puts it."

"Hmm, must be nice." I had a pinch of envy imagining how easy her life must be. "So, I don't know if you have some time this morning or if you mind, but we have our team meeting coming up, and I'd love to get your advi—" Before I could finish, Andre looked up from his desk and interrupted.

"You want me to listen to your pitch?" I nodded, wondering how he knew. "I saw the agenda on Samantha's calendar. Come, darling. Let's go to the conference room to review." He slanted his head and peeked his eyes above his glasses. "And darling," he paused, "you don't have to be so shy. If you need help, just ask."

—

"Is that espresso?" I asked Andre, noticing he wasn't drinking tea like usual.

"Mhm! I came in extra early today. And good thing. I saw a lot of interesting emails come through." Andre raised his voice and sipped his espresso. I knew he wanted me to ask more.

"Oooh, anything interesting?" I exaggerated my intrigue.

"Well, since you asked." He sipped his espresso again. "The head of marketing at Henry's arrived early from Europe and wants to meet *this* week for the pitch instead of next." I shoved any reaction I wanted to make back inside. I didn't want Andre to shut off from sharing more. "So, today's meeting is pretty important. That client lead spot is open, you know." He took another sip of his espresso and widened his eyes. I knew what he was insisting. I just wondered if I was worthy of the role, especially with Natasha having been here longer than me. Before I could spiral, Andre continued, "You need to show her what you got. Stop letting Natasha tell you otherwise."

"What do you mean?" His comment caught me off guard.

"Oh, please. It's so obvious that girl is jealous of you." *Was it that obvious?* "If you're not going to stick up for yourself, at least show out your work. Now let's go, sweetie. I don't have all day here." I recited my pitch, but in the back of my mind, I remained flawed. Someone else noticed what I had all along. Natasha *is* competing with me.

—

An hour later and my Outlook calendar alerted me it was time for our meeting with Samantha. I grabbed my laptop and headed to the boardroom. I quickly checked my phone to see if Adam had texted me back—nothing. I had let him know I wanted to see him again too. *Guess he's just busy with work,* I rationalized.

I turned my attention toward my pitch. Albeit nervous, I was ready to show Samantha and my colleagues what I, maybe, was made of.

Entering the boardroom, my chest tightened, and my breathing sped up. I always got this way before presenting. No matter how many times I've done it, I still put immense pressure on myself, knowing a room of people got a free ticket to judge me, my looks, and my ideas.

I took a seat in the corner of the table toward the back of the room. I wasn't bold enough to sit dab in the center or the front. I watched my colleagues walk in. My hands felt clammy as I held them in my lap. I was relieved when Natasha sat two seats over from me. This way, she couldn't look directly at me while I presented.

Andre set up the projector as another colleague dialed into a conference line. "Can you hear us?" he asked.

"Yes, we're all here!"

"Okay, great. Just waiting for Samantha." Without missing a beat, she arrived, taking a seat at the head of the table. Knowing the client would be here this week instead of next, I was surprised she didn't appear more stressed. She didn't even mention it. But this was on par with Samantha, who had a knack for keeping matters close to the chest.

"Okay, who wants to start with their idea?" she prompted. I should have volunteered, but my anxiety paralyzed me.

"I'll start!" Natasha offered. As uncomfortable as she often made me, I admired the zeal Natasha brought to work.

"Henry's Gin has a seventy-year history, which should be embraced, not erased. As band tees become a staple piece in our closet and streaming has returned nostalgia to our frontal cortex, let's bring back gin. And—"

Before she could finish, Samantha cut her off.

"That's all great, but gin isn't a staple of the nineties unless you're talking about two centuries ago. Keep the idea but rework it. Kay, what do you have?"

"But—" Natasha tried to defend herself. I also admired her courage, but when Samantha said "enough," she meant it.

I cleared my throat. Without time to internalize my talking points or nurture my nerves, I started.

"As Natasha said, gin is a classic drink with a long history but from the 1920s. And our potential client was born out of prohibition, serving as a go-to choice for those who were 'in the know.' Today, Henry's has lost its chic as a premium drink, yet the appeal of drinking premium is still there. So, how do we bring that appeal back to Henry's?"

I expected Samantha to interrupt me like she did with Natasha, but she remained silent. I looked at Andre and nodded. He took this as his cue to project the photos I'd digitally edited. A collage of diverse, young, and middle-aged patrons at a cocktail hour filled the screen. Guests were drinking clear liquor from teal, optic coupe glasses on a city rooftop during the night. They gathered aside marble high-top tables and sat on modern, curve-shaped velvet couches colored in mustard yellow and plum purple. They dressed elegantly modern and chic.

"To drink Henry's is to be part of a collective legacy of classy drinkers. It's an attainable luxury for anyone drip enough to know it."

"Do you have a printout of this?" Samantha asked.

"Yes." I handed her the proposal I had created.

"Ah, okay, this is good, this is good! It's the 'we' I was talking about." While she jumped ahead to other components of the proposal, including a rebranding strategy and advertisement examples, I continued my pitch. A few minutes in and standing on some positive feedback, I was more confident now.

"The ideal Henry's patron has the class not to announce her drink to the world, but the sophistication to know it's better than your average beverage. In other words, she wants to be 'in the know' but doesn't need you to know it. This," I said, "is the modern-day gin drinker." I let out a big sigh of relief. I finished.

"Hm and revamping their original slogan. I like it." Samantha continued to shuffle through the proposal. The rest of the room was quiet. "But we need more."

I froze. I wasn't expecting her to say that. "Well, I have an advertisement idea," I suggested.

"No, no. I mean, this is good, really good. But we need to translate it into a plan."

"Okay, sure, um—"

"Peter, the head of marketing at Henry's, called. Their sales are down, and they want us to help with their rebrand. He'll be here Friday with his team to hear what we got. Kay, I'll have Andre add you to the meeting. You'll lead the pitch with me."

Amazed by Samantha's compliments, I quickly became concerned with what my colleagues thought—especially Natasha. Associates never pitched clients, which made it clear Samantha favored me today.

"All right, everyone, thanks for joining. If you have ideas, shoot 'em over to Kay. She'll be leading this effort for now, but it's meaningful for everyone. This is a million-dollar deal, so let's all be supportive." To my surprise, the three client leads didn't push back. They agreed and left the room, seemingly unscathed by my new opportunity.

Samantha pulled me aside. "I believe it's between us and another firm. I think what you've done here is solid, so let's continue in this direction and plan to meet tomorrow." I nodded. "And don't get too excited yet. With good work comes more work."

Back at my desk, I thanked Andre. "I couldn't have done it without you!"

"Don't butter me up. Of course you could have." He brushed off my praise.

—

The rest of the day, I bunkered at my desk. As happy as I was about the meeting, it also meant I needed to put in more time at LaToulle. Usually, that wouldn't be a problem, but I already committed to working two days at Lola's.

I also couldn't rid myself of obsessing over Adam. Because he wanted to see me again, I permitted myself to fall a little deeper into an imagined idyllic scenario, one where he and I could work out. But he still hadn't responded, and I reminded myself I hardly knew him.

"Woah! It's already five!" Andre declared to no one. He often exposed his thoughts without the need for a response.

Sisi wanted me at Lola's before happy hour to go over paperwork and light training since it'd been a while since I worked there. No one ever left LaToulle on time, so I silently slipped off my open-back loafers and laced up my black and white sneakers. Just as I packed my laptop and stood up, I heard Natasha.

"Where are you going?"

On Tap

My face was hot. I wasn't prepared to answer Natasha, so I just stared at her blankly like an idiot. "I don't believe sneakers are in the handbook," she continued.

"Ha yeah, probably not." I hoped if I didn't say more, she would leave me alone.

"So." She paused for a deliberate and dramatic effect. When I continued to stay silent, she pressed on. "Where are you going?"

"Is it any of your business?" Andre chimed in. "You're not her boss." He rolled his eyes before heading to the kitchen to refill his tea. Without Andre as a buffer, I worried she'd push further, but to my surprise, she flashed a forged smile and walked over to one of the client leads.

Leaving LaToulle to work another job felt scandalous, like a school kid going to the bathroom without permission or something. I reminded myself of the reasons why I didn't tell anyone. Pity for my finances, doubt around my workload, the perception I was too blue-collar to collaborate with clients—a sad but true position I assumed some of my classist colleagues took.

I walked crosstown along Central Park South to Lola's. I noticed all the professionals wearing trendy work attire, slick heels, and beautiful designer bags as they slid in and out of the myriad of hotels and restaurants lining the park. Surely none of them snuck out of their office to work a second job.

I only yearned for the day I could be like them, grabbing my black car or shopping at The Plaza for luxury goods valued more than my rent. I admired their elegance, wishing I was heading to a restaurant I could afford rather than work at.

I took a minute outside of Lola's to reflect. This was the first time I'd been here for work, rather than a party or to visit Sisi, in a couple of years. I had a tang of regret—*am I really doing this?*—and a pinch of excitement to both be working with her again and make extra money.

I opened the entrance door to the main floor, which was quiet and only occupied by empty tables and chairs spread across it. The lights brightened all the way, reminding me of when I first came here for an interview several years ago.

"Hey, girl!" Sisi greeted me, her hoop earrings bouncing as much as her fake boobs. She came up the wooden stairs that led to the lounge and her small office. As any other day at Lola's, she wore an all-black outfit with flashy jewelry and a Gucci waist pouch, a tasteful, modern-day spin on an '80s workout video that only she and her blonde extensions could pull off.

"It's surreal being back here again to work."

"I know, it's just fabulous. Come! Let me introduce you to the staff before I get you on payroll." Sisi brought me through the kitchen to meet the unfamiliar staff and reacquaint myself with the tenured ones. Most knew me anyhow because, as a regular, they spoiled me with decadent dishes every time I visited. I imagine it's because they thought I, along with any other woman in the restaurant, was cute.

Fortunately, this is where the affection stopped, because once Sisi took over as general manager, she put an end to any harassment. She actually fired the head chef, who constantly made unsolicited comments to the waitstaff and warned everyone else to "keep it to yourself, or you're next." The inapt reality is that restaurants don't usually have an HR department. Luckily, Sisi didn't put up with it.

After the kitchen, we continued back to the main floor, where two cocktail servers were polishing glasses and gossiping at the bar while the busboys were pacing around, grabbing ice, and stocking the shelves.

Unlike when I first interviewed at Lola's, I wasn't timid this time. I knew the bar inside and out, and making drinks was like riding a bike. I only hoped people wouldn't think I was pathetic for coming back after getting a "real job," as they often put it. But to my delight, they welcomed me into the gossip, which wasn't about accounts or clients, a relief from the uptight environment at LaToulle.

Tonight I'd work the bar until eight. That's when the dinner crowd usually finished, and one cocktail server could manage on her own. All the tips were mine until then, except for the 15 percent I'd allocate to my barback. I also got a free meal, which was a nice bonus.

"You're a lifesaver, Kay!" Sisi told me again at the top of my shift. "Truth be told, I asked Olivia before the whole half-birthday ordeal because she's my only friend without a job, but she didn't even bat an eyelash before saying no."

"Really? You'd think she'd at least consider it." I attempted neutrality again, though I completely understood Sisi's resentment.

"Yeah, seriously," she went on. "As if I'd ever ask her if I weren't completely desperate. Hello! Doesn't she realize I would never ask after what she put me through unless I *really* needed her?" I often forgot what happened between Olivia and Sisi. It seemed like so long ago. "Anyway, at least I can count on you. Let me go grab your paperwork."

"Sounds good. Thanks, Si!"

"No, thank *you*!"

Lola's main bar was long and particularly narrow for anyone behind it. A mirror the length of the bar hung behind the counter, where an array of alcohol stacked on staggered shelves sat in front of it. The shelving blended with the dark blue walls, and propped above were fake white and yellow flowers. The countertop was a light gray marble, and all the bar's accessories were gold. Cohesively, Lola's was very Instagram-able.

"So, Kay, I heard you worked here before. What brings you back?" the cocktail server asked as we waited for guests to come in.

"Sisi needed some help. And, well, the tips don't hurt either." I shrugged.

"I hear you. I just started a few weeks ago, and the money is really good. Which restaurant were you at before this?" She assumed I came back after working at another restaurant.

"Oh, I wasn't. I'm working at a public relations firm." I hoped she wouldn't judge me in some way for claiming tips when I had a "real job," but to my surprise, quite the opposite.

"That's so cool. I have a communications degree and want to get into public relations." We went on to have a fruitful conversation around our career aspirations, a refreshing start to my first shift back.

House liquors on my left, premium and juices on my right. I organized my jigger, mixing cups, and muddler and asked my bar back to restock the wine and popular whiskeys. Over the next couple of hours, I got lost in the work. I chatted with guests about all kinds of things, like the construction outside, recent politics, and current happenings in their life. I found fulfillment in helping some guests decompress after work.

Though it wasn't all fun, I quickly remembered my distaste for cutting fruit, the beer tap spraying me, and the sticky, dirty floormats ruining my sneakers. About two hours in and approximately sixty customers later, I took a bathroom break and checked my phone.

Adam: What are you up to?

Despite wanting to play it cool, since he hadn't answered me in twenty-two hours—*who was counting?*—I smiled and responded without hesitation.

Kay: At a lounge, easing into my Monday evening

Not a total lie. My status anxiety prevented me from sharing that I was cleaning off dried beer from my ankle at a second job I needed to cover my bills.

Adam: Nice. I'll be at a lounge soon too.

Kay: Where?

I assumed he would respond right away again, but he didn't. I elongated my bathroom break by checking my work email and browsing my Instagram. When he still hadn't answered, I knew I needed to get back to the bar. *He'd respond soon, right?*

By 7:45 p.m., most of the guests had left, and I checked my phone again.

Adam: Chinatown.

I wasn't sure how to respond. I was eager to see him again and wanted to keep the conversation moving.

Kay: Fun, what for?

Adam: Come find out.

He sent me the address. Thrilled, I agreed.

Kay: Be there in an hour or so.

I wasn't sure why I mirrored his short text style, but I knew I needed to get out of Lola's immediately. I counted my tips and organized my cash drawer prematurely. I already made over one hundred dollars in cash, and most people paid by card. The allure of quick money reminded me why the dirty floor mats were worth it.

Over the next half hour, I closed out the rest of my patrons or let them know the cocktail waitress would take care of them. I changed out of my black leggings and tank top and slipped into my work outfit and black loafers before finding Sisi to hand in my paperwork.

"Ooooh, he likes you!" she said when I showed her Adam's text.

"Hm, yeah, we'll see about that. You think I look okay?" I stared down at my outfit.

"You look fine!"

"Si! Everyone knows fine is not fine."

"Okay, you're right. You're beautiful, period. And you just came from work, so he should understand."

"Well, except he won't, because I didn't tell him I work here."

"Why? Are you embarrassed to tell him you were bartending?"

"Um, no. I just haven't told him yet!" I got bashful, and at the same time, my phone pinged.

Adam: It's almost been an hour…
where's Kay?

"What are you smiling at?" Sisi asked.

"He's waiting for me. I've got to run!"

"All right, go have fun. He's a cutie, and so are you!"

As I left, I knew I wouldn't tell Adam I just came from bartending. I wanted to be the most desirable version of myself. Someone who owned her own apartment, had a growing and thriving career, and who didn't need cash tips to make it by. Adam was older, successful, and likely had an expensive apartment. Maybe I'd even see it tonight.

Fool's Gold

My stomach clenched when the bouncer outside a Chinatown speakeasy accepted my ID. I became timid about meeting Adam, reruns from our last date playing over in my head.

Inside, the antique sofas, low tables, and vintage light fixtures created an intimate, romantic environment. The space was mostly unoccupied, except for the small DJ stand on the side of the room and an oak bar full of attractive people drinking eclectic cocktails out of earth-toned cylinder glasses, some of them smoking.

I spotted Adam. His peach-colored T-shirt contrasted nicely with his brown complexion as he laughed with another guy at the bar. I hoped he thought I looked good too.

"This is where you come on Mondays?" I asked.

"Hey, you made it," he said, leaning in for a hug. "Um, not usually, but my friend had a set." He looked over to the DJ, who glanced back at Adam, then me, then back at Adam with an eye like, *You picked a good one.* Encouraging, since I wasn't sure my outfit was as nice or expensive as the others around me.

"So, where were you?" Adam asked, taking a sip of his beer. I noticed he was one of the only people not drinking a themed cocktail. I also noticed his Rolex.

"Ah, uptown at a work thing. So, this is a pretty cool spot." I only half-lied before quickly changing the subject.

"What do you want to drink?"

"Hmm, I'd like to get one of these fun cocktails." I pointed to another woman's drink.

"Can we get her a Fool's Gold?" Adam asked the bartender.

"What's a Fool's Gold?"

"A gin drink. You asked me why I liked gin last time, so I'll show you." I found it sweet that he remembered.

Adam turned toward his DJ friend to listen to the music. I waited to follow his lead on a conversation, but it seemed he was more here to enjoy the music, less so me.

"Great music," I said, trying to push my doubts away and spark up something. He just nodded. The more awkward this was for me, the more I continued to drink. In my tipsy haze, I convinced myself Adam was unattainable. I mean, he was right next to me, but I couldn't get through to him. At times I felt awkward with our lack of dialogue, but I focused on his smile and the speakeasy, which I wouldn't have visited otherwise.

About an hour later, his friend's set ended. "Let's get out of here," Adam said with authority. He didn't ask. He didn't inquire. He just paid the bill and took me outside.

"You don't want to say goodbye?" I asked.

"Nah, he's busy. I want to spend more time with you." His words surprised me in the best way.

"Really?" I couldn't conceal it.

"Yeah, of course."

"I'm yours! Where do you want to go?" I was so taken by his flattery that any initial concerns about the night dissipated.

"The question is, where do *you* want to go? Everything is or will be closed around here soon. So, what about my place?" He turned toward me and glanced downward with a devilish grin.

In the cab, I stared at Adam as he stared ahead, the city lights reflecting through the windows. I found him mysterious but intriguing and wondered what he thought of me.

He rented a brownstone in NoHo, without a doorman but with a swing door elevator that took us to the sixth and top floor. Inside, he flicked on the light uncovering some of his mystery. The white walls were a contrast to his dark furniture spread across the maple hardwood floor. Artwork covered all facets of his spacious one-bedroom, and I could have gotten lost in his travel collection, which included an arrowhead display. He also had hundreds of vinyl records and dozens of plants. Plants everywhere.

He placed a decanter on his walnut coffee table and poured us some wine. He asked what I thought of the music and questioned my knowledge of his plant collection. I couldn't help but feel like he was testing me. Like he wanted to evaluate how worldly I was or how suscept my taste in trendy topics may be. One thing not a mystery, however, was his distaste for getting to know someone through traditional conversation.

A glass of wine and a little conversation later, he lifted his hand to comb my hair behind my ear, lightly touching my face as he did. My stomach tingled, and heat built between my legs. Just because we weren't the most rhythmic in dialogue didn't mean we couldn't be physically. For the first time tonight, I was confident about what we both wanted next.

Adam grabbed my hand and pulled me off the couch to his bed. He laid me down, and I welcomed his kiss. Climbing atop me, he moved his mouth from my lips to my neck as his hand slipped under my stretchy work pants. I felt him harden under his tight fitted jeans as his seducing me only seduced him more.

A moment here and we both couldn't wait. We stripped off our clothes and rolled over so that I was on top of him. Kissing, his hands explored my entire backside before he nudged my body toward the top of his bed, where he positioned me over his face. I grabbed his headboard for balance, his tongue magnetic.

In moments, I had a rush of pleasure unlike anything else. Before I could fully enjoy it all, he pulled me back on top of him and entered me. His body larger than mine, I surrendered to his direction and loved every moment of it.

Aside from peeing right after, I don't remember anything else before falling asleep.

I awoke at five-thirty in the morning, exhausted, next to Adam. It was only Tuesday, and I had to go to work on just a few hours of sleep. Worse, without a change of clothes, I had to stop at my apartment first.

Adam was still sleeping. I left so he didn't see what I looked like in the morning. I sent him a text on my way out.

> **Kay:** Had to leave for work, hope you slept well.

"Kay, where were you?" Andre asked when I arrived at my desk.

"It's nine-thirty." I was late, but not *that* late.

"The Henry's team is on their way."

"Wait, what?" I began to panic.

"You heard me. Get your shit together, girl. They'll be here soon." He pointed his finger at me before sipping on his tea, his pinky finger and brass ring in the air.

When I didn't think it was possible to be more disheveled, Samantha saw me.

"Kay! There you are! Henry's will be here in about fifteen minutes."

"Oh, great!" I said, hoping she didn't notice I was internally freaking out that instead of a few days to prepare, I only had a few minutes.

"I'll meet you in the boardroom. Andre—get me printouts," Samantha said.

"Right here!" Andre said, holding up a few stacks of paper.

"Lovely!" Samantha took them and walked back to her office. I longed for the day I embodied her calmness.

In the kitchen, I drank water and made an espresso. I was exhausted and needed to distract myself before the pitch. Otherwise, I'd psych myself out. Fortunately, distraction was easy, because I couldn't stop thinking about my night with Adam since I woke up. Specifically, the sex. The provocative, orgasmic sex. I've experienced a couple of dozen men, but nothing compared to how aroused my own arousal made him. My body shivered every time I thought about it.

Maybe it was because of this I couldn't help but conflate our sex with my feelings. Adam enjoyed traveling, cooking, music, and had the money to enjoy it all. What would I bring to the table? And could I keep up?

Before I could dwell, Andre let me know the Henry's team had arrived.

"Kay, darling! Boardroom!" he voiced to the kitchen.

Hopefully, while I led a pitch on how to sell their gin, they wouldn't smell the lingering of it on me.

Neat

——

"Try not to get nervous again," Natasha snickered as I walked to the boardroom. I politely smiled, as if she were doing me a favor or something, when I really wanted to ask, *Why do you always want to drag me?*

I had confidence in the substance of my pitch but was insecure about how I looked. With less time to get ready this morning, I was *not* in my best outfit, and my hair was messier than usual.

In our all-white boardroom, I glared at the only pop of color while waiting for everyone. A portrait of a martini glass with a lemon twist hung in the back of the room and overlooked the board table surrounded by twenty-five oversized, white chairs. *How did I get lucky enough to be here, working at the best public relations agency in the industry?*

I always had an admiration for the sophisticated appeal of liquor, even before I drank it. There was something seductive about watching TV characters like Don Draper pouring bourbon in his office or Carrie Bradshaw ordering a cosmopolitan at a chic bar. To now be part of the team that helped curate cultural drinks in time capsules—think a mint julep in the 1920s, a dry martini in the 1960s, or a kamikaze in the 2000s—was fascinating to me.

Samantha's entrance broke my thought. She chatted lively to a tall man with salt and pepper hair and a mustache to match. I assumed he was Oscar, the head of marketing at Henry's. In his gray suit and crisp white shirt, he sat down, two younger professionals trailing behind him. He flipped through a printout of my pitch, and I felt my chest tighten.

"This is Kay," Samantha introduced me. I was seated on the other side of the table and wasn't sure if I should walk over for a handshake or not. But when no one from their end got up, I mustered up an awkward wave instead.

"Kay will be leading today's meeting," Samantha continued. *What?* I knew I was part of the meeting, but *leading* it?

"Oscar, I know you don't like to waste time, so Kay, take it away!" I took Samantha's cue and projected my PowerPoint on the screen behind me. Images of vintage Henry's bottles displayed in rotation, including a photo from a 1920s speakeasy and a still from a 1930s black-and-white film. Then, I kicked off.

"Henry's has a legacy longer than most liquor brands. While many new liquors entering the market are attracting a growing share of consumers, there's a yearning for nostalgia your competitors can't tap into. Think about the popularity of movie remakes, fashion resurgences, and recently social media handles dedicated to decades of the past. Your competitors can't emulate any of this the way Henry's can."

I felt my chest loosen. I took a breath and continued convincing their team that "retro is fashionable." I tried to get a read on Oscar and his colleagues, but their stoicism prevented that. I looked to Samantha for some type of reassurance. She nodded in confidence as if to say, *Keep going.* So, I did.

"Let's capitalize on your capsule of history." I moved to the next slide, which read, "What Was, What Has Always Been, and What *Still* Is," the words displayed around a Henry's bottle with a sepia-toned filter.

"I like this. This is good," Oscar finally spoke up.

"Thank you," I said. "While this photo is nice and captures the essence of Henry's, you could still ask, *What separates a pretty image from others?* Well, this isn't just an image to place on your website or in print ads." I continued the slides to show murals of the bottle and slogan plastered across buildings. "Henry's adds flavor. It's part of our DNA as a culture, a society, and even today in the age of social media." I fast-forwarded to a photoshopped slide of middle-aged tourists and influencers taking photos in front of the street murals. "Henry's has always been a distinguishable luxury brand. Today, everyone wants luxury as much as they enjoy the nostalgia. Your next campaign can hone in on this."

I went on to share my vision for a social media campaign, product placements, and cocktail recipes. I ended the presentation with two words on a slide, *Still Henry's,* and exhaled a sigh of relief. Even if we didn't land this—what I should be most worried about—I was just happy to finish the pitch.

"Ray, Sasha, what do you think?" Oscar asked his colleagues, revealing their names for the first time.

"I like it," Ray said.

"It's intriguing," Sasha added.

"Kay—that was her name, right?" Oscar asked Samantha. "You did well. We recently cut ties with our marketing agency and need a new one. We have a slew of ad buys we need to fill and, more importantly, a one-hundred-year anniversary party to throw. The latter is critical, and the space you showed us in that photo is perfect. Do you do events too? Can you find us a venue like that?"

"Of course! I have a few ideas in mind," I fibbed.

"What are they?"

"Um…" Without an actual restaurant in mind, I didn't know what to say.

"Oscar—give us a few days, and we'll get back to you. Let us confirm availability, staffing, and all the boring stuff," Samantha intervened. With her expertise in handling clients, I should have known better than to suggest something I was unsure about.

"That works," Oscar responded. "We're rushing to meetings all day, but Sasha will connect you with our legal team so we can get a contract together."

"Just our speed." Samantha stood up. The Henry's team rose, and I joined them, this time meeting each other to shake hands. Samantha opened the boardroom door and asked Andre to walk their team out.

"Great job today. You should be proud of yourself!" Her praise was rewarding, as it got my hopes up that she'd consider me for the client lead role.

"Thank you! I worked really hard on it." I wanted her to know that.

"And it showed. But as I say, with good work comes more work. We need to hit the pavement on this rebrand, with a focus on their anniversary event. I'll get legal on the contract stuff. I just want you to find a venue like the one in your presentation. We may need more hands-on-deck for this one." A wave of excitement rushed over me when I realized I'd be working directly with Samantha. But *more hands-on-deck*? I wanted to do this on my own.

"And by the way," she continued, "you've been comfortable as an associate, but I see a lot of promise in you. I want you to use this opportunity to gain some confidence in yourself. Ultimately, we want Oscar asking *you* his questions directly, not *me*." I nodded in agreement. Sure, Samantha was the owner, but there was no reason I couldn't muster up an executive presence that would increase a client's desire to liaise with me directly.

"Thank you, Samantha." I wasn't sure what else to say.

"Don't thank me. You did well. Go grab yourself some lunch."

So I did just that. I bought falafel and rice from a halal cart a few blocks from the office. I sat on the ledge of a water fountain and watched the business executives walk by. I imagined which neighborhood they lived in and what they did for work. I wondered if they could command a room like I wanted to.

La La, Lit

Over the following weeks, I was neck-deep in work and waist-deep in Adam. Aside from my two weekly shifts at Lola's, I spent most of my free time with him. Despite us falling into a new routine together, we continued to fall short of meaningful conversation. I still didn't know what he was looking for or how he really felt about us.

I did, however, know that we spent many evenings exploring new parts of the city together—like roller blading in Prospect Park or watching an old film at a restored cinema in East Village—typically followed by dinners at new restaurants, which he paid for, before I slumbered at his apartment. He planned it all, and like a puppet, I said yes. My guaranteed orgasm, or two, was so irresistible I didn't even want to pretend I was hard to get.

But while we had an undeniable physical attraction, hypnotic even, we still hadn't found our footing elsewhere. Like how I still sensed Adam was evaluating me. He'd often ask if I'd heard of a new trend, budding artist, or the latest AI technology to gauge how much I knew. Or how our conversations fell flat, especially when he brought up topics like these when I'd prefer to talk about personal growth or philosophy.

I wondered what he really knew about me. He still hadn't visited my apartment, and my better sense assumed he'd fallen into situationships like this many times before. Nonetheless, I avoided any effort to entertain these red flags and allowed myself to be love spelled by his chivalry and spontaneity. I focused on the pieces of him I did get to know. He had a lot of friends, preferred cold mountains over hot beaches, and was easily distracted by music, often exiting our conversation prematurely when he heard a song he liked.

Outside of Adam and my shifts at Lola's, I threw myself into building a PR plan for Henry's. I worked hard on the one-hundred-year anniversary event, including curating a guest list and drafting communication materials. However, there was a glaring problem I didn't anticipate—finding the right venue.

Henry's had a specific vision, the one I pitched them, which limited my options. Even more, a diplomat convening would take place the same week, so everything had been booked months in advance. By Friday, I had exhausted all my efforts, and Andre, who helped me call various venues, was fed up.

"Kay, this is absurd. You need to tell Samantha there's nothing out there and offer to host it here or something." My refusal to tell Samantha came from an impulse to show her I could handle this on my own, though I was no longer sure I could.

"Here?" I pointed to the floor. "You mean at LaToulle?" There was no way we'd host it here.

"Well, I don't know that you have very many options, Miss Kay. I think you need to take the L and tell Samantha there's nothing out there." Andre rolled his eyes, and I couldn't blame him. He'd been gracious enough to call around for me but wasn't someone to tolerate an issue Samantha didn't assign him for too long.

"I've got to run, but I'll keep working on it," I promised. As determined as I was to figure this out, I had to leave for Lola's. Just as I grabbed my oversized faux-leather laptop bag, Natasha sat down at her desk.

"What's all the commotion over here?" She always butted in when she sensed something was wrong.

"Oh, nothing, just having some venue issues," I revealed more than I needed to.

"Well, what about Charlie's on Grove?"

Was Natasha actually trying to help?

"Called them. They're booked," Andre said, annoyed.

"I have a short list of places we've had client events before. I can email it to you," Natasha offered.

"No, that's all right. I'll find something over the weekend." I did not want her name on this.

"You should take that list, sweetie," Andre insisted. I imagined Natasha loved the dynamic at play here.

"Okay, sure. Just send it over."

"Well, I don't have to if you think you have it figured out." Of course she was going to dangle the list before me now. Without time to cajole her offer, I dismissed her and threw my bag over my shoulder to leave. "Just kidding! I'll email it," she retracted.

"Thanks." I was short with her but didn't care. I left for Lola's without another word, assuming she and Andre would have a gossip session about me. It was one of the first times my annoyance superseded my need to be liked so much so that I didn't worry about what they thought about me leaving at five today.

Lola's main floor was mostly empty, aside from a few lingering lunch guests. The music played softly, and the lights shined brighter than they would for the dinner shift. The waitstaff and Milo were huddled over Sisi, sitting at the bar with her laptop. I was given permission to arrive later than the others because of my work circumstance. I'm sure it bothered some people, but hopefully not too much.

"What's going on?" I asked everyone.

"Sisi is a star!" one of them cheered.

"Apparently press was here during the jungle party and wrote about it in the *New York Moxy*!" Sisi said. The *Moxy* was a well-circulated digital magazine covering important happenings—restaurant openings, new trends, and contemporary culture shifts—across big cities.

"Get out! That is amazing!" My compliment set off a symphony of praise from the others. "Yo, that party was dope," a busboy chimed in. "We made guap that night," a bartender added.

Seeing how successful Sisi was without a college degree made me question why I didn't skip college myself. Here I was, busting my butt for tips, while she was landing media coverage and about to join one of the city's most successful restaurant groups. I was proud of her, don't get me wrong. I just hoped my corporate career path would offer as sweet a reward one day too.

"All right, all right. Thanks, everyone. Let's get back to work. We have a busy night ahead." Sisi quickly changed the subject, as she often did when the attention was on her. The waitstaff scattered to their respective stations and prepared for the evening. Milo lingered.

"Sisi, I'm almost done with the floorboards, but I noticed there are a few loose shelves behind the bar. Want me to fix it?" he asked.

"Yeah, sure, whatever you see! I can't have things falling apart around here."

I recognized the subtle scent of Milo's cologne as he walked past me and behind the bar. I watched him roll up his sleeves, showing off his chiseled arms. *Was I attracted to Lola's handyman?*

"Kay! Stop staring at Milo," Sisi said right in front of him. Though Milo laughed, I blushed and gave her a look like, *How could you?* She quickly dismissed me.

"One of my guys called out. Can you close the bar tonight instead of managing? There's a small party coming in. It will be easy money."

"Oooh, for sure!" Adam hadn't made any plans yet, so I was happy to opt for cash tips instead of a potential date.

Sisi reviewed the notes for the night as Milo began hammering. She shouted over him that we had no calamari, to sell as much white wine as possible, and the party would be about fifty people. When she finally finished her spiel, Milo stopped.

"Seriously? Are you trying to piss me off?" she asked him.

"Huh?" Milo asked, genuinely dumbfounded.

"Ignore her. She's on edge," I reassured him. "Hey, by the way—question for you," I asked Sisi, hoping to divert her anger.

"What's up?"

"I need to find a venue for an upcoming work event. Think classy meets youthful. Anything in mind?" I knew Sisi was well versed on this and prayed she had a solution for me.

"You're standing in it. Why not host it here?" I should have known she'd say that. She never passed up a business opportunity.

"You know, I really don't want to mix my two worlds like that."

"You're so weird." She couldn't understand why I kept Lola's from my colleagues. "Wait, hold on." Her phone was ringing. "Let me get this." Sisi walked toward the stairs and down to her office.

"Hugo's," I heard Milo call out. I turned to face him. "Hugo's is a great spot for your work event." I tried to recount if I'd heard of Hugo's before. Milo must have mistaken my silence for annoyance at his eavesdropping. "Sorry, I just heard you two talking and—"

"No, no! Thank you. Tell me more about the space. I don't think I've heard of it." He took out his phone to show me photos. He'd been working over there too. "We're almost finished up, see," he showed a video of the near finished space. As he did, his shoulder met mine, and I smelled his cologne again. Subtle but sexy.

To my luck, Hugo's was similar to the idyllic venue I shared in the pitch meeting, including floor-to-ceiling windows surrounding a bar and lounge overlooking the city.

"It's in NoHo. You can tell they're not fully open yet. The ground floor is still being worked on, but the upstairs space is finished. They're planning a soft opening in a few weeks, so maybe they'd be willing to host you. I can ask the manager if you want."

"Ah, yes, yes, please!" I grabbed his arm, unable to contain my excitement.

"All right, all right. No problem." He laughed. "And does this mean I can get your phone number?" If I wasn't mistaken, I'd think he was flirting with me. I nodded and added my number to his phone.

"Lucky me," he smiled. *Okay, he's flirting.* I got nervous and ran to the liquor room, pretending I needed to stock my bar for the night. Instead, I checked my phone. Still nothing from Adam, but an email from Andre.

> **Andre:** Natasha's list isn't too bad. I left
> voicemails for each venue. Hopefully, we'll
> hear by Monday. You're welcome.

Kay: Thanks, Andre, but I got a lead. Will know soon. Fingers crossed!

And with that, I put my phone away to focus on Lola's for the next few hours. No Andre. No Adam. No problems.

Last Call

With the party settled in, I didn't have much to do. I stood behind the bar aimlessly until Sisi rushed up the stairs, looking less than ecstatic.

"Look at this." She held up a pair of earrings and a men's belt.

"What is that?" I asked.

"Olivia and Bryan left this the other night."

"Wait, what?"

"Yeah, I know," Sisi said in disbelief. "I found out from one of the bartenders that she came back with him the night of her half-birthday. They slept together downstairs."

This wasn't too out of character. Over the years, after late nights of drinking, staff members and managers would sleep at Lola's occasionally. It was easier and cheaper than taking a cab home, especially if they had to work the next morning. But Olivia didn't work here, and neither did Bryan.

"Yeah, apparently, she locked herself out of her apartment, and she probably thought it was cool to stay here. Pretty reckless! I told her investors have been in and out while they evaluate my promotion. I could kill her!" Sisi spiraled. I understood why but didn't have the words to respond. I just held my mouth open in shock. "She already jeopardized my job before. I won't let it happen again."

"Totally! I know you two have your history," I consoled her, unable to defend Olivia. It was hard to understand why Olivia perpetuated a pattern of taking advantage of friends. "Maybe I can try to talk to her," I offered. I wanted to do something to help the situation because Sisi and Olivia had been friends, albeit on and off, for many years.

"Good luck with that. She'll be here within the hour, but I don't wanna see her. Hope it's all right I told her that you have her stuff behind the bar."

"Does she know she can't stay here?" I asked, hoping I wouldn't have to tell her.

"Oh, she knows. I made it clear."

It was surprising that a girl as beautiful and fun as Olivia could be so inconsiderate. I suppose that was one of the downsides of having access to anything—lack of boundaries.

When Olivia did arrive, the party had mostly cleared out, and I started cleaning up. She took a seat on the far-right side of the bar, away from any remaining guests.

"Hi, do you have a wristband?" I attempted a joke to cut any potential tension.

"Please, they're lucky to have me here," she answered. I fake laughed, the kind you regret right after because you know it sounded phony.

"Here! Si said you left this." I handed her a bag with the earrings and belt.

"Ah, yes, I just love, love, love those earrings. Didn't want anyone here to take them." She sounded defensive. At the same time, the last guests ordered a round. After pouring their martinis, she looked up from her phone.

"So how mad is she, anyway?" she asked.

I was convinced Sisi had made up her mind about their friendship but didn't want Olivia to feel bad about it. "Well, you know how Sisi can be," I said. To no avail, it still opened up a can of worms.

"I do know! She takes everything so personally. Who cares that I slept here? It's *so* not a big deal." As typical, Olivia was reluctant to admit she'd taken advantage of a situation. I almost said something this time. Almost.

"Well, maybe you can talk with her. I'm sure you two will work it out. I know she cares about you." I shouldn't have led Oliva on, but I worried about hurting her feelings.

"I knew you'd see it my way." But I didn't see it her way. "Anyway, I could use a drink."

"Sorry, Liv, but the party is private." I would have suggested she go upstairs, but I knew Sisi didn't want her at Lola's, period.

"Oh please, no one notices me. And Bryan just told me he wants a break. I didn't even know we were dating! Why would he need a break?" Her change of subject roped me in. I figured a glass of the white wine Sisi wanted to get rid of might be okay.

Olivia stayed and complained about Bryan. She played it like they were casual when I knew she really liked him, exemplified by her rambling about their situation. The entire time I was anxious Sisi would see us. But to my surprise, about thirty minutes later, as the party cleared out, Olivia got a text.

"Can you believe Bryan wants me to meet him for dinner?" she asked after reading the message. Her attempt to sound irked masked her authentic joy.

"It's eleven o'clock. Who is he eating dinner with?" I asked, only to remember it was a Friday, and he wouldn't be at the club until at least one in the morning.

"They're grabbing a bite before Tap," she said, referencing a popular club downtown. "Should I go?" I knew she wanted to, and I needed her out of Lola's, so I nodded wide-eyed and vigorously.

"Okay, I'm going!" With two air kisses and a final sip of wine, she left. Shortly after, I was ready to do so as well. Downstairs, I gave Sisi my cash out. She didn't look too pleased.

"She's not allowed here again," she said sternly.

"No, I know, I know, I just felt ba—" Sisi cut me off.

"It's always a sob story with that girl. I can't have her here anymore. It starts with her sleeping here, and who knows where it ends. She almost jeopardized my job last time, and I have too much on the line now. She's lucky I didn't tell the bouncer to get her out of here." I knew she meant it.

"I get it. I'm sorry I didn't tell her twice to leave."

"And she's not even our friend! When was the last time you two spent time together that wasn't at a party or bar?" I paused, unable to recall a time. "Exactly." Sisi proved her point.

That night, with no plans and no work the next day, I stayed a little longer at Lola's. After Sisi calmed down, we caught up over a drink, and I told her about my dates with Adam. I had no new messages from him on my phone but took comfort in knowing a night with my best girlfriend was better than a text.

Iced

Restarting my phone. Disconnecting then reconnecting to Wi-Fi. Even sending a test text to my mom. Nothing sped up the message I desperately wanted to receive. I told myself it was important I hear from Andre or Milo on the venue, or Sisi with my work schedule, or heck, I would have even loved a message from Olivia about her night with Bryan. But within, I knew I really only wanted one from Adam.

I hadn't heard from him since I left his apartment last Thursday, and I began to spiral. *What did I say on our last date? Was my double bun hairstyle a dealbreaker? Did a wild pack of dogs maul him?*

Not wanting to be paralyzed by his silence anymore, I did exactly what I shouldn't. I swiped on my dating app to find a date over the weekend, knowing all too well another person wouldn't help. And I was right—the date was awful.

When I got home and googled all the ways to deal with someone ghosting you, like how to redirect your attention or soothe yourself mentally, none of it worked. Negative thoughts permeated my brain like a tattoo.

In an effort to further distract myself, I used extra tip money to visit the new Met exhibit, get a facial, and indulge in a swanky brunch—but none of that worked either. With each passing hour, my spiraling worsened.

By Monday, the silence was deafening. I walked into LaToulle thinking how precarious our emotions are—a few weekends ago, I was radiating. Today, I questioned my worth. I donned a long black sweater and leggings, minimal jewelry, and a sour face to reflect my mood.

"Kay! How was your weekend? Any luck with my venue list?" Natasha asked when I sat down, more animated than I'd seen her before. And definitely too enthusiastic for my mood.

"Thanks again, but I have a lead. If I need anything, I'll let you know." This was a lie. I would not be asking her for help.

"Okay, well, Samantha is calling a meeting for the client team this morning, and she'll want an update." I wasn't sure if she was attempting to intimidate or help me. Knowing her, I assumed the former.

"Thanks for the heads up." I remained calm externally but had a gut-sinking feeling internally. Without official confirmation from Milo, I'd have to confess to my team that I didn't have the venue locked in.

Then I realized Andre had been quiet since I arrived, which wasn't like him. *Great, like I need another reason to want to curl up in bed today.*

"You're not mad at me, are you?" I asked him.

"Oh gosh, Kay. Get over yourself. I have more important things to think about," he responded, which almost certainly confirmed he was mad at me.

"If you're so busy, maybe I can help by making you tea?" I asked in an effort to console our situation. Andre looked at me with a curious frown, which I assumed meant he'd take my offer. A few moments later, hot tea in my hand, I saw my colleagues heading to the boardroom, including two assistant vice presidents, three client leads, and Natasha.

I dropped off Andre's tea and hurried to the boardroom. When the meeting started, and I still hadn't heard from Milo, I assured myself everything would be okay. *Right, I'll just be honest.*

A few minutes in and my phone buzzed.

Unknown number: Kay, how are you?

I didn't recognize the number but saw whomever it was still typing.

Unknown number: It's Milo from Lola's. I got the okay from Hugo's.

"Yes!" I said under my breath, but apparently loud enough for others to hear me.

"Do you have something to share?" Samantha asked as if my voiceover was the biggest inconvenience of her day. "Actually, yes, please do share. What's up with the anniversary event? Natasha mentioned she's been helping you out with a venue." *What? Why would she say something to Samantha?*

"Um, no. Well, yes." I was ill prepared for her question.

"Well, which is it?" Samantha asked. Her directness made me nervous, but I rallied whatever dignity I had and pushed back.

"There's an international assembly in the city that week, so it's been difficult finding a place, but I have it covered now."

"Covered how, Kay?" Samantha asked with skepticism. I peeked at Natasha, whose evident glance and slight smirk suggested she reveled in this.

"Well, um, there's a new restaurant opening in NoHo, and, um, we've been approved to host the event there. The space, well, I think, the space looks similar to the one I showed during the pitch." *Okay, not the most confident, but a start.*

"Is this a space from Natasha's list?" Samantha asked.

"No, it's through a friend."

"So you haven't seen it yet?" Samantha pressed.

"Not yet, but I can ask for a walk-through this week if you want!"

"Not what *I* want. It's what *we* need. Get that on the books tomorrow. We need to get moving."

Phew. Her reaction was not as bad as I anticipated. I shouldn't have such high anxiety because Samantha generally liked me, but the pressure of a looming promotion got to me in situations like this. I had an overpowering need to prove myself.

"Natasha, I want you on the event too," Samantha followed up. *What? Why?* "Help Kay with the food, waitstaff, and signage. You know, all the logistics. Kay, I want you to continue focusing on the branding and creatives. Let's make this event unforgettable!"

Natasha and I nodded. I couldn't believe Samantha had asked Natasha to help me, but there was no time to sulk. I continued with my update that I made good progress on the invitations, communication materials, and event decorates, which impressed Samantha. Yet my mind couldn't release the self-doubt I harbored from not having a venue in advance. If I had, I bet Natasha wouldn't have been tapped to help me.

After work, I headed to Lola's for my Monday bar and manager shift. I stepped over the raised floor that divided the office from the lounge. Inside, Sisi was more anxious than usual when I asked about my schedule.

"It's not ready yet! Sorry, I'm just wrapping up a few things. I hired a new bartender, and she's training tonight. Trying to see when I can get her in," she said, shuffling through alphabetized boxes of paperwork. On her desk sat a slick, silver laptop and rhinestone stationary. I remember when I worked here years ago, the office was chaotic and dirty. Now, Sisi's personal touch provided a more inviting and chic space.

"So, are you still seeing that Adam guy?" she asked, taking a break from her search.

"Your guess is as good as mine. Haven't heard from him since our last date on Thursday. Who knows. He's just, um… It's just… Whatever, it's complicated." I didn't buy my own justification, and Sisi wasn't convinced either.

"He's not complicated. He's a player," she said assuredly. Almost too assuredly. "Okay, look, I wouldn't get too involved because you're looking for a relationship, and I don't think he's anything more than a fuck boy." I raised an eyebrow, unsure where her word dump was coming from. "Uh, okay. Adam was here yesterday to pick up his check, and he was with another girl," she confessed.

"What?" My stomach sank for the second time today.

"I know. They were holding hands, and, uh… He's awful." She looked up to the ceiling as she recalled his visit. "He even had the audacity to get dinner with her at the bar! I mean, the dude knows you and I are friends."

I went blank. Adam didn't owe me anything. We weren't *together*, but that didn't prevent me from feeling let down.

"I hate to tell you this, but better you know sooner than later. He's not a keeper." I didn't have the heart to say anything more because her words hit me like a ton of bricks, like it always does when you learn the person you're interested in is not nearly as interested in you. "I'm sorry, girl."

"Ah, what are you gonna do?" I replied, replaying my initial hesitation to go out with him in the first place. "I just should've known." I paused, thinking about our dynamic more. "I mean, we always meet on his schedule, where he wants, and only sleep at his place. The convenience I provided is so obvious. Why would I even let myself think it'd be something more?"

"Because he takes you all over town! And the sex is great. You can't forget that, Kay! We've all been here. Just don't let him get the best of you. He shouldn't live rent free in your head, girl. You gotta kick him out!" Sisi's support made me giggle.

"Ugh, you're right. Why is dating the worst?"

"Tell me about it. I went on a date yesterday, and he told me he only dates girls from ivy league schools." She rolled her eyes. "Can you believe that? I'm surprised he didn't run away when I told him I didn't go to high school."

"Wait, but you went to high school," I said, confused.

"Of course I did! Oh my god, I was joking with him! But he didn't find it very funny. I mean, come on—who doesn't find me funny?"

"Seriously, screw him!"

"Already did!" Sisi admitted, and we both laughed. Her lightheartedness always struck at the right time.

Smoky

A crowd slammed Lola's. I worked my butt off, and luckily it reflected in my tips. Undeniably salty about the Adam news, I grasped onto anything positive, like my ability to service a packed bar adequately and quickly. But as I made rounds and rounds of drinks, I kept thinking about my last morning with him.

Laying on his smooth gray sheets, I watched Adam sleep before I got up, my urge to kiss him rescinded by my fear he wouldn't reciprocate. In an attempt not to wake him, I slinked out of bed to start what had become my "sleeping at Adam's" routine. With no clothes, toiletries, or personal items at his apartment, I succumbed to using his men's body wash in the shower and a splash of water to cleanse my face.

My reminiscing was quickly disrupted when I saw Olivia sitting at the bar. Her look was more combative than friendly.

"Don't worry, I'm only here to let you know I'm not allowed here anymore, and don't act confused," she said. "Sisi messaged me this weekend that she's banning me from Lola's. I know you work Mondays, so I'm letting you know and hope you're not offended about it." She crossed her arms and waited for my response. I got a sense she wanted me to mend the tension between her and Sisi. Why else would she show up here—where she's banned—to share this with me? But it'd all gone too far, and now I was beyond uncomfortable.

"Well, Liv, why don't we talk about this outside of here? It's packed, and I'd rather do this when we have proper time." I tried to express compassion, but two guys were waving their credit cards at me, wanting to order. "It's so busy," I reinforced. "Let's talk later? I'm sure you two can patch this up."

"Oh, please! She needs to take several seats. That girl didn't talk to me for almost a year after our last fight, and it wasn't even that serious!" I was surprised to hear Olivia so casual about it. I remember their situation being much more heated.

A couple of years ago, Sisi found out her mom had an accident during a work shift. She was the assistant manager at the time, so she asked Olivia, the closing bartender that night, to lock up the restaurant. Olivia followed through, but not until five in the morning, after inviting her friends to party, drink free liquor, and snort lines off the bar. All of it caught on camera.

The next day, they fired Olivia, not that she cared, but Sisi almost lost her job. In fact, if it weren't for that incident, Sisi would likely already be an investor. To this day, an icky blemish remains on their friendship.

"Well, maybe she'll change how she feels. Let's find time out of here?" I pushed again, hoping Olivia would leave.

"Yeah, whatever. What are you doing this weekend?" *Does this girl not know how to take a cue?*

"I'm working here and on a big case for wor—"

"Boo! Bryan is throwing a huge bash again, and we wanted you to come."

"Sounds fun, but work has me swamped!" I tried tending to the two guys waving their credit cards, obnoxiously now as they desperately fought for my attention.

"But these parties are lit! So lit, Bryan's hosting them monthly. Come to the next one?"

"Yeah, sure. It's a plan." I faintly committed.

"All right, well, I'll let you get back to," she paused and looked down at the bar covered in garnishes and empty glasses I wasn't able to clean yet, "well, all of this." She gave two air kisses and squeezed through the crowd to leave. *Phew.*

The next hour I tended to at least a hundred people and made a multitude of drinks. When I finally took a bathroom break, I checked my phone to see a dozen unread emails, a missed call from Milo, and what I'd been waiting for all weekend—a text from Adam. Seeing his name jolted me and diminished any joy I reaped from my other notifications.

> **Adam:** Kay, where have you been?

His line was cheesy, outplayed, and above all, annoying. My elation fell to melancholy. I didn't know what I expected from someone like him. I felt dignified knowing he still wanted me even if he did have a Rolodex of girls on hand.

I just wasn't sure what to reply, so I texted Milo instead.

> **Kay:** Hey, you called?

> **Milo:** Come by Hugo's tomorrow afternoon. Manager will be around.

> **Kay:** Sweet! Be there around two.

Then I responded to Adam.

> **Kay:** I've been waiting to hear from you.

I regretted it the moment I hit send. While it was honest, I didn't want him to think he had me wrapped around his finger. Because he did.

On the Rocks

My rose-colored glasses blurred my emotional vision the next day at work. Adam had been texting me since last night, even making plans for us to go to a concert in Astoria tonight.

When I couldn't justify a reason to go, other than the stroke his attention gave my ego, I texted Sisi, hoping she'd justify one for me.

> **Sisi:** When someone shows you who they are, you need to believe them. Don't compromise your standards just because you want a relationship.

I should have done just that, but technically, Adam hadn't done anything wrong. We weren't exclusive. If I wanted to know what he was looking for, then I needed to ask him myself, which I planned to do tonight.

I'd also be clear about what I was looking for and flout any fear of coming across as desperate or clingy. I even wore my favorite office-to-evening attire in preparation. A white, scoop neck blouse, easily maneuverable to an off the shoulder top, maroon booties, and dark, wide-legged jeans that cusped my butt perfectly. I put on long, thin gold earrings and a few rings that competed with Andre's. I felt confident in my outfit and eager for my evening in it.

But before any of that, I needed to visit Hugo's for the walk-through. Unfortunately, now that Natasha was helping, she'd also be with me.

"You look cute. Are you dressed up for this walk-through?" she asked as we waited for our rideshare.

"I actually have a date tonight." I didn't care that I usually shielded my personal life from her. I needed to practice directness before my night ahead.

"Oh, with whom?" she asked as the rideshare pulled up. On the way over, I told her about Adam, that he's a DJ, handsome, but also a player. That my friend recently saw him with another girl, which guaranteed he didn't take me as seriously as I wanted him to.

It was probably naive to divulge any of this to Natasha, given we hardly talked, but I couldn't stop myself. I wanted to talk about him to anyone who would listen.

"Who knows, maybe he could be the real deal. But stay guarded," she opined after my divulging. I was warmed by her support, a nice glimpse into what a possible friendship could be. That or I was desperate for compassion.

"Yeah, guess we'll see." I shrugged.

"I've been dating, too, but it's hard to find someone who wants to commit," she added. It was the first time in almost two years of working together that she disclosed anything about herself. The friendly side of me wanted to ask more, but my better instinct knew not to. After all, Natasha had just told Samantha I needed help on this account, which is why we were sharing this car ride in the first place. So, I kept it surface level.

"I know, the guys in New York are awful."

"The girls too." Natasha pivoted her head from the window to me. "What? Didn't expect me to be into girls?"

"Not even," I replied. "I'm just surprised that—"

"That we're even having this conversation?" She laughed. "We need an escape from work once in a while, right?"

"Right." I agreed hesitantly. Outside the white walls, we were better able to shed our office shell, but this was uncrossed territory, and I wasn't sure we were ready to go there.

Moments later, we pulled up to a brownstone on Park Avenue. The building looked more like a luxurious multilevel apartment than an event venue. Inside, the bottom floor was under construction but served as a massive entryway for gathering guests, passing cocktails, and photo taking. A spiral staircase penetrated the center of the room and led up to the top floor.

"Hey, is anyone here?" Natasha called out. We looked around, then at each other, before hearing a giant slam that made us both jump. A second later there were footsteps, and I saw Milo appear at the top of the stairs. *What is he doing here?*

"Hey!" He waved and walked down toward us. In typical fashion, he wore paint-stained jeans, worker boots, and a white shirt hugging his chiseled arm muscles.

"I didn't know you'd be here," I said.

"Ah, yeah. I'm working here today, so thought I'd come in a little early to introduce you to Fernando, the manager." As nice as that was, I just hoped he didn't bring up Lola's. I didn't want Natasha advantaging professionally off me more than she already had. "Let me take you upstairs. It's still a little dumpy down here."

Milo took my hand. Unprepared, my heart sped up a little, his grip confident yet gentle, his hand softer than expected for a handyman. I wondered what Natasha thought of this as she followed behind us.

At the top of the staircase, Milo released my hand and nudged me to walk on the floor space first.

"Shut up! This place is unreal!" I gushed, blown away by how stunning the venue was. Elegant, modern watercolor furniture, woven pendant lights, and overgrown monstera plants furnished the room. Floor-to-ceiling windows opened up to a view of the Lower East Side. It looked brand new, which was completely unexpected, given the construction below us. Up here was the perfect rendition for the *exclusively attainable* vibe I was looking for.

"I knew you'd like it." He smiled, impressed with himself.

"It's incredible!" I stroked a couch and awed the view.

"It's nice, but is there another way to get up here without the stairs? And where is the bathroom?" Natasha asked, interrupting mine and Milo's moment.

"The restaurant is wheelchair accessible. The elevator is over there." Milo pointed to the right side of the room. "And the bathroom is actually behind here. Let me show you." He brought us to a wall jutted out in the far corner. Behind it was an open sink area with four doors to private bathrooms.

I looked to Natasha for her reaction. I knew she had a few years of experience in event planning before LaToulle, and she seemed to be asking the right questions. "All right, so the essentials are covered," she said.

But why is she leading this walk-through? I needed to take command.

"When will Fernando be here?" I asked.

"He just texted me. He's running a few behind."

"All right, let's check out the bar then," I suggested, knowing this was one part of a restaurant I was an expert in.

We waited at the sleek, black countertop positioned in front of the oversized windows. The liquor shelf hung low behind the bar to avoid disrupting the view. But the entire bar was small and wouldn't cater to a large party. I wondered how we'd make it function during the event.

"Do you two want a drink?" Milo offered.

"Are we allowed?" Natasha asked. *How juvenile. We're clients. Of course we are.*

"Fernando insists." Milo swayed his hand over the liquor options behind him. I spotted Henry's on the shelf.

"I'll have Henry's on ice with muddled limes." Seemed appropriate to drink the brand we were here for.

"Same for you?" Milo asked. "It was Natasha, right?"

"Yes, Natasha. And sure, I'll do the same." As Milo made our drinks, I anticipated she would ask how Milo and I knew one another, but the opposite happened. The event occupied her, and she was writing a list of questions for Fernando.

"What do you think of the space?" I asked, fishing for some credit.

"It's nice, but there are so many things we need to sort out." Her eyes roamed the room, and she jotted down more notes.

"Here you go, ladies. Fernando is coming up now." Milo handed us our drinks. At the top of the staircase arrived a midsized man with a lot of facial hair and slicked-back hair. He wore a dark pink shirt with a green leaf print underneath a royal blue blazer. His socks poked out below his trimmed pants. They matched his shirt. *Quite the outfit for a Tuesday afternoon.*

"Hello, ladies. It's so nice to meet you both." He offered us a handshake, the sun shimmering off his silver watch. "I'm so glad you've decided to host your event here. Come! Let me take you to the kitchen, where we have some appetizers prepared for you." Fernando's presence came across as inviting but forged, like he wasn't as thrilled to be here as he let on. Nonetheless, we followed him to the new, stainless-steel kitchen, where several plates were laid out.

"We are finalizing our menu, so I hope our mini-arepas with pulled pork, avocado crema, Pico de Gallo, red sauce, fried sweet plantains, gazpacho with a tomato base, and dragon fruit salsa will be sufficient for your affair."

"Now, this looks amazing!" Natasha said, glaring at the food.

"Oh, and it is. Try it!" Fernando gestured for us to eat. And we did. We tried each decedent plate, all of it as delicious as it looked.

As I chewed, I wondered how his staff planned to prepare everything in the short time frame we'd be working in. Our guests would arrive all at once, and the fried plantains and mini-arepas were made to order. But when I asked Fernando about this, he brushed me off.

"And how do you know so much about Latin food?" he pivoted.

"It must be all your restaurant experience," Milo interjected. I felt my face flush as I thought about my second job potentially getting exposed. Suddenly, the timeliness of the food wasn't so important.

"Natasha, do you want to go over the run of the show with Fernando?" I proposed, diverting the attention off me.

"Yes, yes, I have a million questions," Natasha said before she and Fernando left the kitchen.

"I'm so glad you like it here," Milo said as we finished the last two mini-arepas. But I dismissed him.

"Yeah. So, hey. No one at LaToulle knows I work at Lola's. I know, kind of weird, but please, can you just keep it between us?"

"Oh, I'm so sorry, I didn't know!"

"No worries! Now you do, so we're good," I reassured him.

"Can I ask why you don't want anyone to know? I think it's pretty badass you have a side hustle."

"Well, thank you, but…" I didn't have a great defense for my secret because I wasn't willing to admit I cared too much about my image at work. That my colleagues may think less of me for sneaking away to a second job that helped afford my world. Or that Natasha would use it as ammo to crush my chance at a promotion.

"That's all right. I won't say anything. But hey, I need to head downstairs. If you couldn't tell, there's a ton of work to do."

"Of course! Thank you so much. Seriously, I don't know what I would have done if it weren't for you telling me about this place." Milo looked at me with a smile in his eyes.

"It's nothing," he said, placing his hand on the side of my arm. Butterflies surfaced as his eyes held mine.

"Kay! Can you come here?" Natasha shouted from the dining area.

"Coming!" I shouted back, Milo releasing his hand and gaze.

—

After reviewing plans with Natasha and Fernando over another drink, I had a slight buzz and was eager for my concert date with Adam. I went straight from Hugo's to Astoria. With some time to kill, I stopped by a bar next to the concert hall. Waiting for Adam, I prepared myself for an honest conversation. *You're ready for a relationship, and there's no reason to hide it.*

But when Adam finally arrived, I sensed the timing wasn't right. Something about the loud music, anticipation of a fun evening, and the uncertainty of whether he'd reciprocate prevented me from saying anything. I worried I might not see him or experience our euphoric sex again. So, we went to the concert then slept at his place, and I awoke early the next morning tired, regretful, and without face wash.

Gin

With only a few days left until the Henry's anniversary event, Natasha slipped back into old habits and became difficult to work with again. She left me off emails and resisted any effort to problem solve, only surfacing issues during our meetings with Samantha. I wanted to say something to her. I thought we'd actually had a breakthrough during the walk-through, but back inside LaToulle's walls, we were right where we started.

Responsible for the theme, including the invitation design, party activities, and decorating of the space, my role was much more visible to Oscar and Samantha than hers. It was finally evident to me that she was, in fact, salty, like during a planning meeting, when she discounted the Henry's mini-bar concept I pitched to Samantha. Natasha scoffed at my suggestion to add one to each table arrangement so guests could create their own signature Henry's cocktail.

Funny enough, Samantha exploded with approval. And so did Oscar when she told him about it. They especially loved that the minibars would ease any overcrowding at the actual bar. It was then no surprise that during our final meeting, I assumed everything was set for the event, only a day away. However, there was a new glaring issue. We didn't have enough RSVPs to comfortably fill the room.

This wasn't because we couldn't find people interested in going—the event was exclusive and free. It was because we needed to find the *right* people. A mix of late twenties to mid-fifties professionals who would appeal to the VIP guests of restaurant owners, influencers, and investors I'd already invited.

Technically neither Natasha nor I had been assigned this task—though if she had met with me beforehand, we could have caught this—so we both made an effort to rally more attendees that afternoon. I invited Olivia, who agreed and would bring some friends. I knew Sisi wouldn't make it and figured this was a nice way to show Olivia that, though Sisi had banned her from Lola's, I wasn't banning her from my life.

I seemed to have slipped into *pen pal* territory with Adam lately—he transitioned from *seeing* me daily to *texting* me daily—so I regretted not using our prior date to ask about his intentions. Not that it mattered too much. They were increasingly clear. That said, I still decided to lean on him for help boosting the guest list. His network in the music scene was part of the core demographic we needed. Not to mention, organizing this event was one of the *cooler* parts of my role that I wanted him to see in hopes it would reinvigorate his interest in me.

Kay: Hey, can you call me this afternoon?

Adam: How about we see each other instead? Come over after work?

Like clockwork, I said yes. I justified that my going over to his apartment would help me at work. The reality was we hadn't seen each other since the concert, and I wanted what I didn't feel like I could have.

On my way over, I thought about our prior dates together—all fourteen of them. Like the night we met at his apartment for wine, half a joint, and sex in his living room. We napped before visiting a quaint club in Brooklyn. The smoky air, neon lights, and cash bar were out of my comfort zone. A night without much conversation, our chemistry captivated me as we danced. Thinking about that night, I had an epiphany. *The only chemistry we had was physical.*

The thought permeated throughout my night with him. I recognized the flatness of our conversation, including my boredom, as I listened to him talk about his new favorite artist. And his lack of interest in the new book I was reading. Yet, I didn't let it deter me from asking him to the anniversary event. I'd already held back my intention on our last date, and I wouldn't do it again.

"Yeah, that sounds pretty cool. I can ask some people I know." I was elated but played it cool.

"Amazing, you'll have a good time," I responded, thinking about how great it'd be to show my coworkers I was dating someone of Adam's caliber.

That evening, after wine and dinner, Adam fell asleep right away, but I stayed awake. My mind raced about the event, Natasha, and mostly over Adam. I harbored on my revelation about our connection only being physical until I finally dozed off, static from the record player continuing on a loop across the room.

My next morning started on a high, knowing Adam would be at the Henry's event. Still wearing my metaphoric rose-colored glasses, I even splurged on a latte and scone for breakfast. I assured myself I wouldn't need to worry about budgeting forever.

Gin Part II

———

Excited about my dress—even if borrowed from Olivia—it was one of the most fabulous I'd ever worn. As difficult as she could be, her generosity was appreciated, even if an excuse for her to show off her clothes. Not to mention, it was Prada, and she'd only worn it once at last year's Tony Awards.

Deep maroon and shimmery under light, the dress was short without revealing too much and fit snugly on my size six frame. It matched a pair of dark brown, strappy heels I owned. Best yet, it provided me with a false sense of financial belonging too. I brushed on eye shadow and shrouded myself in affordable gold jewelry. *You look pretty good.*

I met Natasha at Hugo's. Contrary to me, she looked office professional in a black blazer, slacks, and a forgettable button-down.

"Hey! You ready for tonight?" I asked her.

"Well, not really. It's chillier than I thought, and we don't have a coat check. There's no toilet paper, and the kitchen is understaffed." Her glossed over eyes and look of panic indicated she also came without a solution.

"Okay, well, big yikes. The party is in two hours, and Samantha will be here soon." I shared a sense of worry, but

Natasha had no response. "So, seriously? No toilet paper?" I reiterated.

"Didn't you hear me?" she snapped. "But that's not the issue. My sister will get that. We need a coat check, and we need more appetizers." I didn't appreciate that she said *we* because, technically, these were *her* responsibilities.

"Okay, okay, umm…" I tried concocting a solution, but stress took over as I allowed her attitude to overwhelm me. "Let's print a sign instructing guests to hang their own coats. What do you think? They must have a printer somewhere!" I blurted the first idea I had.

"Seriously? And if someone swaps their Zara sweater for a Gucci coat?" She had a point. But before I could answer, she aired another grievance. "And what is all that noise? Is that construction?" *It must be Milo.*

"Okay, hold up. I have an idea." This time, before I blurted anything else out, I ran downstairs and saw Milo, just as expected.

"Huge favor to ask you." I interrupted him from working. He put down a drill and peered up at me from under the clear goggles protecting his eyes.

"Well, hello to you too." His response was playful, armed with a warm smile. It was amazing he didn't seem bothered by my abruptness.

"Ha. Ha. But seriously, we need help! We don't have a coat check tonight." I looked at him, hoping he'd offer. But he stayed silent, his eyes blank under the goggles. "Would you do it?" I asked before I begged. "We'll pay you! And you might get tips." He stood up to meet me.

"But I've never coat checked." *Is he actually entertaining my proposition?*

"Oh, it's easy!" I showed my best grin in hopes he'd agree. "Did I mention we'll pay you?"

"Mm, you mentioned that. And what else do I get out of it?" He asked in a way that made me think he was flirting again.

"I'll sneak you some appetizers?" I asked with innocence, knowing very well I was playing up my flirtation for help.

"Hmm…" He put his hand on his chin as if I didn't know by now he'd agree. "You have a deal." *Oh, thank God.*

"Ah, thank you, thank you!"

"But," he held up his index finger, "do I at least have time to run home and change?"

"Um, yeah, okay, sure. Well, wait, the event is in an hour," I said, checking my phone. "Where do you live?"

"Like, twenty minutes from here. Williamsburg." *Williamsburg?* As a handyman, I imagined he lived in a less expensive neighborhood.

"Oh, okay. Yeah, no problem. Just please, please be back by seven-thirty."

"Only if you say please again," he joked.

"Please!"

—

Natasha let out a sigh of relief when I told her the coat check problem was handled, yet the stress on her face remained. She brought me to the kitchen, where the staff looked equally stressed. They grumbled at one another in Spanish, which Natasha and I took as a hint to stay clear. We hurried back to the venue floor, where Natasha's sister arrived with toilet paper.

A beautiful woman with long blonde hair and even longer legs waited at the top of the stairs. She wore a heavy, short coat covering any bottoms she was or wasn't wearing and thigh-high black leather boots. She was, in every sense of the word, a showstopper. The staff gazed at her as she walked to us with two large, transparent plastic bags of toilet paper.

"I'd never seen someone look so good carrying toilet paper," I whispered to Natasha, but she just rolled her eyes.

"Thanks, Bri. What do I owe you?" Natasha asked when her sister approached us.

"A new pair of heels! Those stairs go on forever," she responded, handing over the toilet paper.

"Well, like I said, thanks. Just Venmo request what we owe you."

"Yeah, yeah. Just be happy I was nearby already." Natasha replied with a blank stare, and Bri met her with the same gaze. I wondered if this was an unspoken game of chicken but with words.

"Hi, I'm Kay. I work with Natasha." I hoped my introduction would serve as the knife needed to cut the tension in the room.

"Oh, Kay. It's nice to meet you. I've heard so much." She seemed less interested in me and more intrigued by the venue. "Well, at least the place is great," she said, looking around.

"Thank you! Are you staying for the party?" I asked nicely, hoping to also increase our guest count.

"Um, I'll try and swing by."

"Try to?" Natasha snapped.

"Okay, okay. Don't worry. I'll be back here soon," Bri said before heading out. "Bye, you two!" When she walked away, everyone gazed at her again.

"Can you please take this and stock the bathroom?" Natasha handed a staff member the toilet paper, which broke his attention from Bri. Thrown off, he dropped the toilet paper before quickly picking it up and shuffling to the bathroom.

"Geez, men are so feral," Natasha scoffed. I laughed until I saw Milo walk past Bri on the stairs. I think he was the only one not fawning over her.

"Hey! I'm gonna run now. Do you need anything while I'm out?" he asked.

"Milo! You should have left already!" I couldn't believe he was still here.

"Oh, okay! I'm going, I'm going!" He ran back down the stairs.

"Is that our coat check?" Natasha asked.

"Yes, that's Milo. Remember him from the walk-through?"

"Yeah, I do. I just hope he comes back with a clean shirt," she said with an attitude.

We only had an hour and a half until the event. I needed to finish decorating while managing my inbox, which was exploding with questions from Andre. He couldn't attend because he caught a cold but still managed to help by monitoring RSVPs from home. In between liaising between his emails and our on-site happenings, I took a moment to send Adam a selfie of my dress.

Kay: Look forward to seeing you soon.

Gin Part III

With a few minutes until guests arrived, I grabbed one of a hundred identical cocktails, each in a champagne flute, lined up behind the bar. The cocktail included Henry's gin, pomegranate liquor, and a splash of champagne, sprinkled with pomegranate seeds.

Looking around the Henry's branded venue, I had no doubt Oscar would be pleased, especially as the sun set over the Manhattan skyline. Everything completely embodied the vision I pitched a mere month ago. The LaToulle staff were here to help fill the place before the Henry's team and other stakeholders arrived, including the restaurant owners, board members, and influencers.

I thought our first guest walked in, but it was actually Milo. He was dressed in a way that almost made him unrecognizable. *Almost,* because I couldn't mix up his boyish face and brown curly hair for anyone else. He wore fitted dark blue pants, an oversized button-down and, to my surprise, a pair of Vans shoes. Pulled together, his look gave him a skater boy edge. For the first time, I noticed Milo beyond being a handyman.

"What? Wasn't sure I'd come back?" he asked.

"No, no. Um, I knew that. Um, here, come this way." I led Milo to the coat check area when Oscar arrived, carrying his jacket.

"Are we expected to hang these ourselves? Where is the coat check?" Oscar asked.

"Oh, hi, Oscar! Um, you're here early," I said.

"I'm on time." His face was expressionless.

"I'm right here!" Milo interjected. Oscar handed his jacket to Milo, who looked at me like, *All good, I got this,* before heading downstairs. Oscar appeared annoyed before grabbing a cocktail, all while one of LaToulle's VPs complimented me on the mini-bar stations.

"Look at these custom mini-Henry's bottles. Uh, just love!" she said in earshot of Oscar. "How on theme! Good work, Kay!"

Over the next half hour, guests trickled in, including Olivia and her friends. She looked as good as always and was in a surprisingly tame mood. I imagined Adam would be here soon too. I hadn't heard from him yet, so I assumed he must be getting ready. I couldn't think about it for too long because Natasha found me in a panic. This time, she was really sweating.

"What's wrong?" I asked.

"High key, that kitchen sucks. One of the servers just dropped a huge plate of appetizers! It took them about an hour to put it together in the first place. What the fuck!"

"Aren't they short-staffed too?" I asked.

"Not helping!"

"Sorry, let me check on it." I remembered why I tried to warn everyone about prep time during our walk-through.

When I popped in the kitchen, I overheard Samantha, whom I didn't realize was here yet. She was talking to Oscar in the corner.

"Okay, okay. I'll work on it," she said.

"You better! There's no reason we should all be waiting for food! I pay you way too much money to worry about this bullshit!" Oscar raised his voice, which seemed too intense for a small matter, but I supposed he was as anxious as the rest of us.

"Of course, Oscar. We'll handle this. Go back out and enjoy the event." Samantha did her best to reassure him, but Oscar stormed toward the door. In a swift move, I backed up so he wouldn't see me. I then reentered to approach Samantha, pretending I hadn't already heard her.

"Kay! There you are." As always, Samantha looked fabulous. She wore an evergreen, velvet dress, tight fitting at the waist with oversized should pads that were more modern than the '80s. She wore her hair pulled back to show off her oversized floral earrings. "What is going on with the food?" *I don't understand why she's asking me. I hadn't had a hand in the food throughout the whole planning process besides tasting it.*

"Well, Natasha was working on—"

"Kay, we don't have time for that. This is your and Natasha's event. Please get food out there immediately. We don't need to jeopardize one of our biggest clients over tortillas." Even when Samantha was mad, she remained elegant and likable. I just wanted to please her.

"On it." Near the prep stations, I saw the head chef pacing behind his sous chefs, who were curating appetizers at a snail's pace. I couldn't understand why, so when I saw Fernando on his phone, seemingly oblivious to it all, I signaled that I needed help. He just stuck up his index finger, instructing me to wait. I tried getting his chef's attention next, but he ignored me too. *Does no one take me seriously?*

I thought about Lola's kitchen setup. They always had extra food stored in the freezer, either for staff meals or weekly specials. Hugo's was a new restaurant, but surely they did too. I snuck in the freezer, the rest of the staff too busy to notice, and found dozens of mini burgers. I laid them on a table next to Fernando, who was still on the phone.

"What is this?" he asked, finally putting down his device.

"Fernando, people are going through the food too quickly, and your waiter just dropped a bunch of appetizers."

"Ay yi yi! We cannot serve these! Surely our menu is worth the wait." It became clear Fernando didn't want to risk the quality of his food.

"Look! You're understaffed, and the chefs you do have move at a glacial pace. So, while the sprinkles of cilantro are nice, there's no need for perfection. Now please, we've worked so hard on this event, and I can't have the only hiccup be this. Let's just throw these in a microwave and call it a day." I surprised myself with my candor.

Fernando grimaced before shouting in Spanish at his staff. Suddenly, two more chefs came out from behind a second door and jumped into action. *Where did they come from?* "I'll be sending you a bill. Those were supposed to be for the staff." He had an attitude like it wasn't his fault in the first place.

—

Once the sliders came out and the remaining appetizers caught pace, Samantha and Oscar were at ease. I had another drink while mingling with coworkers and spending time with Olivia. I asked her if she had talked to Adam about the event, considering they knew each other, but she hadn't. In fact, she didn't know we'd been dating. "You actually went out with him?" she asked.

I also met someone who mentioned Adam invited him. But when I told him who I was, he had no clue. Worse, Adam still wasn't here. Not even a text. At 9:30 p.m., I concluded he was one of the "no-shows."

Disappointed, it was hard for me to enjoy the rest of the party. I allowed myself to be consumed by what wasn't—no romantic evening showing off Adam to my colleagues—instead of what was—me hosting a memorable event for an important new client and inching closer toward a promotion. Not wanting to bask in self-pity, I went to find Natasha and see if she'd settled down too. I walked downstairs to check for her but only saw Milo.

"Have you seen Natasha?" I asked him.

"Nope! Been neck-deep in coats." Behind Milo was a completely full coat check closet.

"I hope they're tipping you!" Milo held up a jar of ones. It looked like he amassed no more than forty dollars, so his overenthusiasm was cute.

Back upstairs, Samantha stood with investors and LaToulle board members while Oscar mingled with the restaurant owners—exactly how I envisioned it.

—

Before the event ended, Oscar stopped me. "Kay, right?" He was still unsure of my name. "Nice job tonight. Especially on the food. The mini burgers were a nice touch to the more decadent apps." I could have laughed, but I opted for a simple thank you instead.

When he left, Samantha came up to me next. "Everything was fantastic! The minibars and overall aesthetic were superb. Thank your friend who helped us find this place. It's spectacular." I beamed at her compliment, nearly forgetting about my disappointment over Adam.

"I'm so glad you liked it!"

"You've got a knack for this, Kay. We just need to work on those logistics. But we can talk about that at the office." She was referencing the food. "Enjoy the rest of the night. I'm going to chat with Natasha before heading out. Ah, there she is!" Natasha passed us, and Samantha followed her into the kitchen.

I scrunched my nose and thought about eavesdropping. *You really shouldn't.* But I couldn't help myself. I snuck into the kitchen, where I overheard Oscar and Samantha earlier.

"We can't have shit storms during go-time." Samantha sounded like she was laying into Natasha.

"I know, but we got the toilet paper right away!" Natasha defended herself.

"Bri shouldn't be doing that for you. I told your aunt I'd hire *you*, not your sister." *Samantha knew Natasha's family?* "Anyway, let's go over it all later, and if I were you, I'd thank Kay for saving things tonight. You could learn a thing or two from her." I quickly ducked out of the kitchen to avoid being seen.

With Oscar and Samantha gone, I took a seat at the bar watching the few lingering guests and Olivia finish their drinks on the floor. Then, Natasha sat next to me.

"Where were you?" I asked as if I hadn't just overheard her conversation in the kitchen.

"Ever feel like you can have everything and nothing at the same time?" I wasn't sure if it was the drinks, the relief that comes with finishing a big project, or Samantha's comments, but Natasha was vulnerable again.

"Funny you should say that." Natasha treated my words as an invitation to continue opening up. She shared how she'd been living in the shadow of her older sister Bri, even following her from Montreal to New York.

"It's like I have something to prove to my parents when really I just want a wife and farmhouse in Canada."

"If that's what you want, then what are you doing here?" I asked, accepting her vulnerability with some empathy but mostly pity.

"I guess I'm trying to prove I can be as good as Bri. Not sure why, though. It's not like she ever came back here tonight. She's too cool for my world. I don't know why I ever thought she'd support me." I wanted to tell her the same thing happened to me, that Adam told me he would show up too. But I knew better. Natasha was vulnerable now but could very well be closed off tomorrow.

"When someone shows you who they are, believe them." I passed on the advice I really should've been telling myself.

"Hmm, isn't that the truth." She let out a sigh. Then, Olivia approached us.

"Kay, we're gonna keep the party going at Tap. Bryan is hosting. You should come!"

"Thanks, Liv, but I need to do a few things here. If I can join later, I will." It was nice of her to invite me, but I'd been dodging her invitations a few times now and hoped she'd get the hint that my club days were seldom.

"Ugh, you'll never come!" She walked away, and I realized she never complimented me on the party or thanked me for the invite.

"Who is that?" Natasha asked.

"Ah, a friend from Lo—" I stopped myself before almost revealing I worked at Lola's. "Ah, just a friend."

"Hm." Natasha grunted. I sensed she was judging my and Olivia's friendship, which gave me the urge to defend it.

"Yeah, I know, she's a lot. But at least she showed her support by coming."

"Or she just wants a party." Natasha shrugged. I wasn't sure if I was talking to her or Sisi. Apparently, Olivia's narcissism was so obvious even Natasha picked it up within a minute of meeting her.

"Well, we can give ourselves a pat on the back, right? At least it wasn't a total disaster," I said, hoping she may reveal what Samantha said in the kitchen. But she didn't, and I didn't have it in me to call it out.

I got up to leave but paused at the top of the stairs. I turned to reflect on the venue behind me. I admired the city lights glistening behind the vast windows, the twenty or so remaining guests continuing to dance, and my Henry's mini-bars tousled from guests making drinks on them all night.

Adam not coming didn't reduce the effort I put into this event, nor was it lost on me that everyone who *did* show up came for something I put together. I smiled and mentally patted myself on my back, since Natasha wouldn't. *You did this, Kay.*

I headed downstairs to get my jacket. Just before reaching the bottom, I got a text.

> **Adam:** Hope your party went well. I couldn't make it, but you can tell me all about it in bed later.

His text didn't warrant a reply. He'd been showing me who he was. It was about time I finally believed him.

After-Party

___

At the bottom of the staircase, I saw Milo on his phone, guarding the few remaining jackets in coat check. I sat next to him and slipped off my heels, my feet aching from wearing them all evening.

"How'd you make out down here?" I startled him.

"Oh, hey, Kay." Milo looked up from his phone, seeming a little nervous.

"It's all right. You can be on your phone," I joked, assuming he was cautious not to be caught with it while *working*.

"No, no, it's not that. I just didn't, um… I didn't think I was going to see you again tonight." *Huh?*

"Yeah, I'm still here," I said, awkwardly. "But leaving soon! I'm exhausted."

"So tell me, how was your night?" It was nice to have someone care after the whirlwind event. So nice, in fact, that I spent twenty minutes telling him all about it. About Natasha, the toilet paper, the appetizers, and everything with Samantha. I stopped just short of telling him about Adam. I didn't want to associate my successful night with his absence.

"And tell me about Lola's," he followed up after my rant. "Why do you work there?" I shared my career timeline. How

I left Lola's for LaToulle's, only to come back and help Sisi while earning more money. That I was up for a promotion at LaToulle and felt pressure to earn it, so I'd hopefully have an *option* to work at Lola's instead of feeling compelled to.

As Milo and I sat together, the rest of the crowd left, including Olivia. When she walked by, I hid behind the coat check door to avoid her. Milo laughed and pretended I wasn't there when he handed over her coat.

When I came out of hiding, Natasha walked down the stairs as the last one to leave. She simply waved at me before walking out the door. I guess she was ready to call it a night too.

"All right, enough about me, geez. You must be so bored!" I said to Milo. I felt guilty for only talking about myself. No matter how well Milo listened, I was sure he was ready to get away from me.

"No, no, it's really all right. I was actually supposed to meet someone tonight, but it's too late now."

"I'm sorry! How annoying of me to keep you here."

"Not at all. I'd much rather be here." I was happy he'd rejected my assumption but wasn't convinced he meant it.

"Here?" I pointed to the floor in disbelief. "I can't imagine this is more fun than whatever you had planned." Milo laughed and put his head down bashfully. "Well, seriously, don't let me keep you," I continued. "You've done enough to help us out tonight. I said thank you, right?"

"Only a dozen times. Happy I could help." We both smiled.

"Guess we should get home now." Once I said it, I knew it wasn't true. I didn't want to go home. I really enjoyed being around Milo and wanted to learn more about him.

He maneuvered himself from behind the counter that divided us. He gave me a strong hug, the scent of his cologne as aromatic as earlier.

"It was nice being here with you. Let's do it again when we're not both working." Butterflies fluttered in my stomach, knowing full well that, this time, Milo was, in fact, flirting with me. Unprepared, I pulled away, acting as platonic as possible.

"I've got to let Fernando know it's a wrap!" I waved like a dork, and walked briskly toward Fernando's makeshift office, unsure if he'd even be in it. *Could I be any more awkward?*

—

I received no shortage of compliments the next day at LaToulle. Though Natasha led the event logistics, it was clear to my higher-ups that I was the lead. For once, I was more than just the girl who *supported* their work. I actually *ran* a project on my own.

Andre noticed too. He and I were writing thank you notes to the attendees. "Kay, everyone is talking about the event! You killed it, darling!"

"Aw, thank you! We missed you! But I'm glad you're feeling better."

"I would've missed me, too, but no one needed me coughing everywhere. How repugnant." Andre glowered. "Okay, so tell me *everything*!" As we worked on the handwritten notes, I told him what everyone wore and how they behaved. Adam's ears must have been ringing, because just when Andre asked who didn't show, I got a text from him.

Adam: Hello? What's up?

His message a follow-up to the one I ignored last night. Admittedly, it bummed me out that he never showed up, but his thoughtless text made it easier to move on. However, I wouldn't ghost him the way several guys had done with me. Even if Adam deserved it, I had the dignity and growing courage to let him know exactly *what was up*.

> **Kay:** Thank you for the fun times and new adventures. I'm looking for a relationship, and I don't believe we're a match for that, so I think it's best we stop getting to know one another. Best of luck.

After I hit send, Samantha called her staff for an impromptu meeting. She wanted to review upcoming activities, recent client updates, and, of course, last night's event. As always, I was nervous about the meeting, especially knowing I'd get feedback on it—from everyone, in front of everyone.

When we got to the end of the agenda to discuss the event, I acknowledged the venue should have been locked in earlier and the guest list completed sooner. But this was minimal, given how well everything turned out.

"Kay, you did a wonderful job at capturing the concept we're selling Henry's. Now that you've had a go at this, I'd like you to strategize our branding work moving forward. You've got a knack for this." I relished in Samantha's request, which also drew me closer to a title change.

Still beaming, it was hard to worry about the subsequent feedback she provided Natasha. "Let's come up with an event checklist, so pieces aren't missing moving forward," Samantha asked her before the meeting ended. I'm sure Natasha was upset, but personally, I wanted to dance out of the room.

Samantha grabbed me before I could. "Kay, follow me to my office."

"Coming!" I tensed up, unsure what Samantha could add after the meeting. While she'd just complimented me, I lived in constant fear of displeasing her.

"I want you to go to Austin this weekend for their Food and Wine Festival. I can't make it, but I think it's good you're there to scope out what's going on. We've always worked with traditional liquor brands, but these days there are so many new concepts coming to market. We need to blow everyone out of the water this year, and I trust your judgment! You're already on the guest list. Andre will send the confirmation today."

"Oh, wow, yes, sure!" I'd never been on a work trip with LaToulle before and was honored Samantha wanted to use *her* budget to send *me* somewhere.

"Keep in mind, Austin is quirky, eccentric, and young. Don't be afraid to use what the city has to offer as inspiration," she said. "No one knows who you are down there, so try and make new connections too." Kind of harsh, but she had a point. I wasn't a *somebody* in our business... or anywhere, for that matter.

Back at my desk, I texted Sisi.

> **Kay:** I got asked to go to Austin this weekend for the Food and Wine Festival. Any chance you can find coverage?

> **Sisi:** No way! Was thinking of going to that. How fun! And yes, got you covered.

> **Kay:** Thx! I can work extra next week if you need me.

Sisi: That's fine, Kay. You can take time off without owing any favors. You're allowed that.

I was, wasn't I?
Then, my phone pinged again.

Adam: Just because we're not compatible doesn't mean we can't still have sex.

My stomach dropped with disgust. He officially warranted no response. I had better things to think about, like my weekend in another city.

Cosmopolitan

Riding my postevent high, I arrived in Austin a few days later on my first work trip with LaToulle. The Food and Wine Festival would feature a number of new liquor brands, and I was eager to check them out. Especially because LaToulle's board wanted to diversify our portfolio to better appeal to younger audiences.

Even better, Sisi surprised me by joining the trip. Apparently, Lola's was on the Food and Wine Festival's radar after their feature in *Moxy*, and Sisi was asked to attend. Another manager from a sister restaurant covered for her, absolving us both of our restaurant duties. The only caveat was my flight was full, so Sisi booked the next one and would arrive a couple of hours after me.

On the plane, I purchased in-air Wi-Fi for the first time and ordered a snack. It was a foreign feeling to know everything would be paid for by work, but one I could get used to.

Stepping out of the airport, the dry air contrasted with the spring breeze in New York. I took a deep breath and felt free from strife. Austin was my invitation to detach from the bar, the office, and Adam.

My taxi was cleaner and drove slower than any in New York. Nearing downtown, I noticed palm trees sprouting from the sidewalk along an enclave of dive bars. The streets were full of people sipping beer and listening to a myriad of outdoor music.

My hotel sat in the midst of it all. A bellman greeted me, another foreign feeling as I'd never had someone offer to carry my luggage before. Growing up, my parents considered gluttonous cruises or the Holiday Inn a luxury.

Assuming the bellman would want a tip, I politely declined his gesture and carried my own bag up the entrance stairs. The lobby looked like any other, except for oversized musical instruments hanging from the wall and ceiling, which reminded me I was in Austin, a city that celebrated live music wholeheartedly.

I showered to rinse the filth of flying. I sat on the crisp, white bed sheets in my standard double room. I looked around at the impersonal décor—the brown furniture, plastic coffee machine, and used channel sheet on my bed stand.

I picked up my phone next to my packed suitcase. No new messages, no new emails. Aside from the muffled noise in the street, the room's silence fell on me. I sat there wanting to maintain an excitement about the trip, but everywhere I looked was a reminder I was alone. Totally alone.

I laid my back down on the bed. I had a choice—I could sulk here until Sisi arrived or get out and make the best of the city. I chose the latter. I threw on a pair of jeans, a T-shirt, and my cross-body bag. Down the street from my hotel was the Texas State House.

After a short line and minimal security check, I entered the large, dome-shaped room with high ceilings. Along the rounded wall were portraits of prior Texan governors, all of whom were men, except for one.

There has been one woman governor in Texas's history, and I wondered what gave her the drive to rise above expectations and enter a competition among men to lead her state.

She sat poised yet relaxed with a face that read, "I'm here, and I matter." I wondered where she developed the independence to believe her ideas were worthy of being heard, approved, and enacted. How fortunate we can stand on the shoulders of women like her, who made it possible for us to live our modern-day truths and ideals. Surely, if she could earn the governorship of Texas in the early twentieth century, I could make a name for myself in the corporate world.

I pocketed this nugget of inspiration before scoping out the sea of restaurants and bars downtown, all of which were more inviting than New York's. Here, I didn't see any velvet ropes indicating exclusivity for the wealthiest or most notorious. I did, however, see some dodgy bars with older men. Wanting to avoid unwanted flirtation, I sought out a chic, cactus-themed bar.

"What're you havin'?" the bartender asked when I sat down. Tattoos ran down his arms, and he wore a short-sleeved plaid shirt and baggy jeans.

"A Diet Coke and a menu, please." I wanted to order fries but also planned to wear a slim-fitting dress later, so I opted for a side salad with shrimp instead. Tempted to check my work emails, I reminded myself I had my "out of office" auto reply set up and didn't need to. I opted to read the news instead.

It was then someone sat next to me, her personality bubbly as she talked to the bartender. I became distracted by her British accent and lime-green pantsuit. I tried not to linger on her outfit, but it was so distinct from anything I'd seen since arriving in Austin that I couldn't help myself.

"Hey, I'm Lilly," she introduced herself. She must have noticed I was staring.

"I'm Kay, and I knew you couldn't have been a Texan."

"The accent gives it away, huh?" She flashed a pearly white smile that contrasted beautifully against her dark complexion. "I'm a Brit, but I live in New York."

"Ah, I'm from New York too. I'm here for the Food and Wine Festival."

"You don't say! I'm a journalist and I'm here to cover the Food and Wine Festival." I knew better than to ask what outlet. Typically, when New Yorkers kept their jobs vague, it was to avoid revealing they worked at a prominent institution. It was the not so humble, humble part of our identity.

"I'm with LaToulle Relations. We're a PR firm for liquor brands." Unlike a big corporation, not everyone knew of LaToulle unless they were in the industry.

"Ah, Samantha LaToulle, very cool." I was surprised she knew of us—well, knew Samantha. After more small talk, I learned we'd be at the same event later—a *Pink Party* hosted by a new beverage brand.

"Here are your fries." The bartender handed Lilly a stack of fries smothered in gravy and cheese. I suddenly regretted my order, and I think she could tell.

"Want one?" she offered. We shared the basket and talked more about Austin and our favorite neighborhoods in New York City until I got a text that Sisi arrived.

"I'll see you at the event!" I said to Lilly before meeting Sisi back at the hotel room.

—

"Okay, let's talk options!" Sisi instructed, referring to our potential outfits for the Pink Party. "You'll have to tell me which top goes best with my new lip gloss."

"Wait, are your lips *bigger*?" I asked, noticing they were plumper.

"Yes! I didn't think anyone would be able to tell. I just got filler last week, but I think the plane made them swell!" She walked over to the mirror and lit up with contentment. "Ah, they're huge!"

Without responding, I checked my phone. This was the first day since the anniversary event I hadn't received a desperate text from Adam. I didn't want to talk with him but took comfort in knowing he was still trying.

"Hello? Do you see how great these look?" Sisi asked again, pointing to her lips.

"Huh, no. Sorry, let me see," I asked, distracted as I scrolled through mine and Adam's previous messages.

"Can you get off your phone? We only have a short time until we leave." I put my phone down.

"Is it that Natasha girl again? What happened now?"

"No, no, it's not her."

"Good, because we can't have her ruining our trip."

"Ever feel like you can have everything but still feel so alone?" I asked, reciting the same line Natasha asked me at the party.

"It's called a vibrator, sweetie."

"Ha. Ha."

"Kidding! Is this about Adam? Kay, that dude is not worth your time."

"No, it's not even that. It's just the feeling of being alone."

"Kay, he sucks. The sooner you focus on what you have going on that is positive, the better off you'll be. Plus, I'm here!

And I need you to get out of self-sabotage mode to help me get ready. Now tell me, how great do my lips look?"

Thirty minutes later and we were ready. Sisi truly fit the bill. She had on pink latex booties that wrapped up to her knees, an oversized, off the shoulder pink tie-dye T-shirt, and no pants. Her wavy blonde extensions were long and flowy.

"You look great! It's giving Barbie meets pop star vibes," I told her.

"Perfect!"

"What bag are you wearing?"

"This one!" Sisi held up a pink latex box-shaped bag. "What about you?" I showed her the pink baguette I brought.

"Love it! Now get your shoes on. I need a drink." I slid on bright pink shoes with a transparent wedge, which contrasted with my fuchsia corset and three-quarter-length, wide-legged pants.

The party kicked off the official launch of Brunch in a Bottle, a canned nonalcoholic beverage brand. In my research, I learned their team aimed to sell themed mocktails, like mimosas, Bloody Marys, and Bellinis, in ice buckets at boozy brunches across the country. Thus far, they'd only had a soft launch but performed strongly, in large part because it resonated with young people who've been quitting drinking in droves.

Knowing LaToulle's board wanted to expand our audience, I was keen on convincing their team that we could blow them up. As for Sisi? In addition to her love for a good theme party, she also thought they might be a good fit to sell at Lola's.

—

The festival took place in a field several acres wide. Clusters of vendors under white tents took over, and I couldn't identify where they ended. A diversity of guests representing various industries and professions swarmed the place—some in business attire, some in hipster wear, and most in casual, posh clothing.

Once Sisi and I were in, we spotted several attendees in pink and presumed they were headed to the Pink Party too. As we followed them, I noticed how attractive and styled they looked and was glad I coordinated my outfit. It relieved some of the impostor syndrome I may have felt otherwise.

A black stanchion blocked the only pink tent in the field. It appeared we were attending the only exclusive party in Austin, yet no one was there to guard the entrance.

"Maybe it's just for optics?" I asked Sisi, hoping there wasn't a guest list.

"Hmm, maybe." Unfazed, she lifted the rope to let us in. Apprehensive, I looked around to see if anyone saw us, but I didn't see staff anywhere. I followed Sisi, closing the rope behind me.

"Miss! Miss!" A few seconds later, a rambunctious woman wearing a black suit flailed behind us. Her lanyard indicated she worked here.

"This event is for invited guests only. Do you have an invitation?" A few of the other attendees stared at us as she stormed at Sisi and me with a scanner in hand. *Great, just the entrance we needed.*

I didn't know what to say. We hadn't been invited, but I absolutely needed to go to this event. I had planned my pitch for days.

"Um, I don—" Before I could answer, Sisi stepped in.

"Excuse me, but I'm Sisi Schwartz with Lola's Lounge and Bar. Part of LAR hospitality. Is there any reason we can't attend?"

"Yes, ma'am. This is by invitation only."

"Well, I don't have one." Sisi acted like her response was enough to justify our entrance.

"You *cannot*, under any circumstances, enter without it." It was a humbling reminder that we were not, in fact, very important people. As Sisi and the young woman entered a stare-off, I saw Lilly coming our way.

"Abigail, you can let 'em in! They're with me." Abigail reluctantly let us through. Mortified, I thanked Lilly. Her long black hair, slicked back in a tight ponytail, paired gorgeously with her pink pantsuit. She looked equal parts chic and professional.

"Oh, it's nothing. She can be a real arse! I'm just glad you're both here. And what great outfits you've got on!" she said before leaning in for a double air kiss with Sisi.

"You two know each other?" I asked, pointing to Lilly and Sisi.

"Of course!" Sisi said. "Lilly writes for *Moxy*. She interviewed me for the feature on Lola's a few weeks ago."

"No, no, sweetie. That feature was about *you*! I was so impressed with how you've resuscitated that place. It's one of my favorite spots in town these days! It's a delight to see you here." Lilly took us to *Moxy*'s table with her colleagues, all of whom *were* invited. On the way, we passed a flower-themed photo booth and stilt walkers sprinkling rose petals above the crowd.

But none of this distracted me from why I was really here. I needed to meet the Brunch in a Bottle team. I just wasn't sure where they were.

"Honestly, I find the Brunch in a Bottle concept pretty interesting, but they need a new name. How drab!" Lilly said about an hour into the party. She, Sisi, and I were taking photos in the flower-themed photo booth.

"Right! Hopefully, they hire my firm, and we can help them rebrand," I said as we held up flower props.

"Boozies or something catchier," Sisi chimed in before we took another photo.

"Right! This isn't even a bottle!" Lilly said as we took our last photo. "Hey, do you see that woman over there?" Lilly asked after we left the booth.

"No, who?" I turned around.

"Don't be so obvious!" I turned back, embarrassed. "Okay, look again, but more discreetly. She's wearing the pink blazer." This time, I saw the woman Lilly referenced. "She's the marketing director for Brunch in a Bottle and the one you're going to want to talk with." I nodded before scoping out how best to approach this woman.

I envisioned myself getting tongue-tied or tripping on my way over. Then I thought about not speaking with her at all. Not being able to tell Samantha I landed us a potential client… That was scarier.

I combed my hair with my hands, adjusted my corset, and walked up to the woman in the pink blazer. "Excuse me. Hi." She looked puzzled. "Hi, sorry, I'm Kay with LaToulle Relations." The woman's expression changed from uncertain to appealing.

"Ah, the renowned Samantha. You work for her?" she asked.

"Um, yes, I do."

"Ah, lucky girl. She's a legend. What do you do for her?"

"I'm a client lead. I focus on creative branding and marketing for our clients." This was only partially true. While I'd worked on Henry's the past few weeks, I was only an associate and by no stretch resolved of my administrative and entry-level work.

"Well, Ms. Creative, I'm Myra, and it's lovely to meet you. Tell me, what do you think about Brunch in a Bottle?" This was my moment to tell her what I'd been brainstorming.

"I love the concept! Seeing how younger generations are increasingly moving away from alcohol but still enjoy going out, I think it's a hit! And the flavors, they're good. But I do find the packaging and branding need work." I surprised myself with how little I withheld.

"Well, tell me what you really think!" Myra laughed.

"I really believe you'd be a great brand for LaToulle. There's so much we can do to build off your initial success. With a few enhancements here and there, I see Brunch in a Bottle going national. Just like that!" I snapped my finger.

"Here's my card. When you get back to New York, why don't you and Samantha give me a call?"

"Of course, we'd love to." *Did I really just do that?* Elated, I headed back to the *Moxy* table, ready to share the news with Sisi and Lilly.

"That is just fabulous, Kay! I know exactly how we can celebrate," Lilly said. "Our team loves you both and wants to invite you to our work dinner." Her colleagues were as friendly and outgoing as she was, so Sisi and I said yes without hesitation.

The dinner was at an oak farmhouse, and *Moxy's* reserved table—longer than LaToulle's boardroom—was set in its backyard. They strung big, bulbed lights above the table and decorated the yard in pink floral to match the Pink Party theme. I emailed a picture to myself as inspiration for a future event.

"Is this a media event or something?" Sisi asked Lilly.

"We're writing a feature for Brunch in a Bottle." I assumed this meant they had good funding—music to my ears.

By the end of dinner, Sisi and I were beat and too full to go anywhere else. In the taxi back to our hotel, the driver played Miley Cyrus. We sang the lyrics in between gossiping about our night. Austin didn't feel so lonely after all.

Inventory

I again took pleasure in my expensed Wi-Fi on the flight back to New York with Sisi. I started writing my Monday to-do list when she bumped her arm against mine to get my attention. I took out my headphones.

"What's up?"

"Look at this photo!" She showed me an image of Lola's newly repaired wall, where the drapes I picked up a few weeks ago had been.

"Who sent that? The repair looks great!"

"Milo. He finally finished. But no, not that! Well, yes, it looks good, but look on the side here." It was Olivia sitting at the bar. "What doesn't she get about not being allowed there?" Sisi shook her phone like she was about to yell at it, her plumped lips pursed like a fish.

"Okay, okay." I pushed her hand down to insinuate, *Calm down for a moment.* "I think she's just bummed that you two aren't friends. Think you can talk it out?"

"Kay, I'm going to need you to realize she's toxic. Tox. Ick." Sisi was right, and once again, my detest for conflict overrode my rationality. I just couldn't shake my soft spot for Olivia. She was one of the first people I met in the city.

"I'm sorry, Si. I know it's frustrating." I avoided discussing their conflict further. I was more excited to hear about Milo. "So, to not so subtly change the subject—does this mean Milo is finished at Lola's? Like, finished finished?"

"He's finally done! I needed him to do a lot, and I'm so glad it's over. He was getting pricey!" I was disappointed to hear I might not see him again. "Wait, why are you asking?" Sisi questioned.

I gave her a look like, *You know why.*

"Ah!" she shrieked. A man across the aisle gave us a dirty look. "I love this! He's so nice and so so, so cute!"

"Yes, he is. But he's also a handyman." I released a phony laugh.

"Oh, gosh, Kay. Who cares? You really need to get over this complex you have. You're so worried about everyone else all the time. What about you? Milo is such a nice guy, and he's hot. Why wouldn't you go for it?" I pondered a moment while the man across the aisle grew more annoyed with our conversation.

"I think that guy wants us to be quiet," I whispered to Sisi.

"And? I'm talking at a normal level. If he has a problem, he can ask for earplugs." She made another good point. "Look, I won't tell you what to do, but he's a nice, hardworking guy. It's about time you dated someone like that."

"Well, if I'm not going to see him at Lola's again, maybe I'll text him."

"You've got nothing to lose!"

So, I did just that before Sisi showed me potential suitors on her dating apps, her long fake nail tapping the screen as she scrolled.

On Monday, I was less anxious about the weekly meeting. Dare I say, I was a little excited to share my trip with

Samantha. Instead of obsessing about what I'd bring to the table, I actively listened to my colleagues' updates. As I did, I realized I could handle their same responsibilities, like managing a disgruntled client or drafting a press release for an expanded product launch.

I kept this outlook when it was my turn to unveil the news about Brunch in a Bottle. My colleagues' feedback was swift and encouraging.

"It's a good idea we start expanding our clientele," one said. "To-go drinks are everywhere."

"We need to hop on that," another said. I imagine they also liked that a growing client list meant larger bonuses.

"I knew I sent you there for a reason, Kay! Send me their website, and I'll take a look," Samantha chimed in. I noticed Natasha's head faced down. It was evident as ever that Samantha favored me as the stronger associate.

After LaToulle, I went to Lola's. But unlike my recent shifts, Milo's absence was palpable. I wanted to see him again but still hadn't gotten a reply to my text.

"What do you mean he hasn't responded?" Sisi was surprised when I told her. I even had to show her the text as proof. "How strange. You're a catch! I think you should text him again. Maybe he didn't get it."

"How desperate would that be!" But I did it anyway.

Kay: Thought I'd hear from you by now…

I then prepared for the shift ahead. Maybe Sisi's advice would work and I wouldn't be *as* single by the end of it.

As the crowd picked up, the motion of pouring drinks and wiping the counter became mundane. Even though I only worked a couple days a week, I remembered why I traded in tips for taxes. While some aspects of bartending were really fun—meeting new people, free drinks, and discounted food—the whole slicing limes and dodging creepy comments got tired.

When I had a chance to check my phone, Milo still hadn't responded. *Maybe the issue really is me. I must have assumed too much and too quickly.*

A few more dinner guests and a decent sized happy hour crowd later, we did last call. I had another thirty minutes to finish cleaning the bar when a customer asked me when I was getting a *real job.* The nerve. I just hoped he got the hint when I shot back, "This is my real job. What do you mean?" I then realized the hypocrite in me to prematurely judge Milo for being a handyman. The irony, because even he didn't want to go out with me.

I turned in my bank to Sisi and collected my tips. I quickly swallowed my sour grapes from earlier when I counted three-hundred dollars. The cash made up for the mundanity of my night and motivated me for my next shift.

On my way home, as I mentally recited my to-do list for the next day, my phone pinged.

> **Milo:** Wow, completely missed your text.
> Of course, I want to see you. Tell me when
> and where.

Finally! My waiting for him to answer only made me more intrigued. I suggested we go out for an early drink on Friday afternoon. It was Cinco de Mayo, and I had the day off from LaToulle as an annual celebratory holiday, one Samantha thought only right to pay homage to.

Mixer

———

Today's call with Brunch in a Bottle had to go well. Earlier this week, Samantha got upset with me after I didn't immediately respond to her "urgent" email—it wasn't—at 5:30 p.m. on a Tuesday. She even requested we "have a talk."

Truth was, I went to the bar early that day because Sisi needed help and Samantha was traveling. I thought I'd get away with it but was wrong because Samantha asked that, moving forward, I always be available before 6:00 p.m., especially in light of my recent client responsibilities.

I hated her calling me out. This was the first time my second job jeopardized my primary job, and I wouldn't let it happen again, even if making five hundred dollars left me wondering if the tradeoff had been worth it after all.

—

"I never imagined Brunch in a Bottle would get here! That I'd work with *the* Samantha LaToulle," Myra admitted on our call later that week. "But I won't lie. We're pretty desirable right now." She let out a laugh.

"Oh, we know!" Samantha responded. "You've got a great product. We've traditionally only worked with established clients, but we believe in your brand."

The call continued on just as positive a note. Myra shared their vision, current challenges, and why they were ready to hire a PR firm, though she was notably more excited to speak with Samantha than me, leaving me to feel like a fly on the wall of a meeting I organized.

"Let us discuss how we can be the best firm for you, and I'll get back to you tomorrow. We want to make this the absolute right fit," Samantha rounded out our call.

"Thank you, Samantha. This is why your reputation supersedes you!" Myra hung up. I waited for Samantha to gush openly about how great this opportunity was. But she didn't.

"Okay, so let's think about this. The goal is to expand their audience. The early twenties to mid-thirties range, right?"

"Right. This demographic is trending away from alcohol and toward mocktails, from traditional brands to new experiences. Even better, Brunch in a Bottle isn't a direct threat to any of our existing clients since they're alcohol-free." I shared my armor of knowledge with Samantha, who I think stopped paying attention. She looked out the window to think for a few moments before turning back to me.

"This is exactly what the board has in mind. We just need to lock it up. Myra's a fan, clearly, but we need to reel her in if other teams are poaching. We might want a client lead on this." Her tone was uncertain. But I knew in my gut I could handle this alone.

"I want to handle this. Brunch in a Bottle already has a following in the Southwest, especially on college campuses and in bigger cities like Austin. I know we can make them a household name across the Northeast, starting with New

York. We have the best pulse on this city and can use our connections here as their launching pad," I pleaded.

"Okay, okay, I like that. But we've also got to change their name," Samantha said, subtly agreeing with my plea.

"I absolutely agree. I actually mentioned this to Myra at the event!"

"Ah, lovely. They must already be simmering on the idea. Great, great." Samantha said *great* when she liked something, so I was thrilled to hear her say it twice.

"Myra mentioned she wants to get Brunch in a Bottle into upscale cafés, like Pink House. It's what inspired their all-pink event," I said.

"Why don't you go there this weekend and scope it out? We can use your experience to curate a list of other venues they'll fit in. And while you're there, brainstorm some creative ideas for our next pitch," Samantha directed. I presumed this meant we didn't need another client lead. "And don't get too excited. Let's see what you can do on your own first." I nodded, knowing I could craft a plan that would not only reel Myra in but would keep her hooked.

Later that evening, I celebrated my work feat with a glass of wine and a new episode of my favorite show. Tomorrow would be a long day. Between my first date with Milo and working Lola's Cinco de Mayo party, I wanted to be fresh and energized. I enjoyed my couch, my TV, and my eagerness for the day ahead.

...with a Splash

Unlike most first dates, I wasn't nervous about going out with Milo. Contrary to my dates with Adam, our conversation had been effortless the few times we were together, and I felt less pressure to impress him.

Milo suggested we meet at a bar in Midtown, which seemed random given it was Friday afternoon and Midtown was mostly quiet. Nonetheless, I went to his suggested restaurant. I pushed a large brass door to enter a dimly lit space, the inside gloomier than the sunny weather outside. Big round bulbs dangled above a long bar where only a few patrons sat. A sole gentleman on one end and two young girls laughing at the other. No Milo yet.

Glancing at my seating options, I opted for a small love seat next to the window, overlooking the street. Waiting, I noticed two servers counting money and rolling silverware in a booth next to the kitchen door. As an experienced restaurateur, I knew they were finishing side work during their lunch-to-dinner lull.

The music played softly over the cream and orange furniture. There was something about an aesthetically pleasing restaurant that elicited possibility. I imagined this place could be very lively if the right crowd and time permitted.

As I moved my attention to the illuminated wire running like a jigsaw inside each bulb and the lead pipes zigzagging along the industrial walls, Milo walked in. He went straight to the bar, unaware I was already there. Like the Henry's event, he wore modern streetwear and a pair of Vans, a departure from his work clothes.

When I saw he tried grabbing the bartender's attention, I got up to let him know I was already here. He was in the middle of his order when I leaned my arm against his. "…straight up, with a splash of…" He paused when he realized I was aside him. He smiled handsomely. "Oh! … with a splash of Kay." He finished his sentence, smiling at his own pun. The bartender looked confused before realizing Milo was being cutesy with me. He sucked his teeth and picked up a bottle to make Milo's drink.

"You were already here? Not fair!" Milo hugged me.

"Right over there." I pointed to the love seat where my scarf lay. "Actually, I was checking out the architecture in here. This place is new, right? They did a great job."

"Ahem, thank you," Milo said proudly.

"Don't tell me this was you?" I asked in disbelief. "Is that why you invited me here?"

"You think I'd bring you to Midtown on a Friday for any other reason?" He went on to tell me how he helped develop the space during his internship two semesters before. That it was actually a factory and difficult to integrate the pipes with the overall design. I looked around as he explained. I saw Milo everywhere.

Over the next two hours, our conversation flowed as effortlessly as the ones before. There were no extra breaths to count or awkward pauses. But the sun shifted West, and my shift at Lola's was starting soon.

"Where's your sombrero?" he joked as a group of people walked by in Mexican-inspired attire.

"Don't remind me. I can't believe Lola's is having a Cinco de Mayo party." I didn't mask my unenthusiasm. "Actually, I probably need to leave soon." I checked the time on my phone. "Oh my god! I needed to leave ten minutes ago." It was unlike my punctual self to lose track of time.

"For Lola's? Already?" he asked.

"Ugh, yes. Apparently, it's a ticketed party, and Sisi sold out. Good for her but exhausting for me."

"So, uh, no sombrero?" he joked again. We both stopped speaking for the first time since we sat down. His face read, *Please don't go.* I assumed mine read similarly, like, *I really don't want to.*

But I had to. Not only would Sisi kill me if I didn't show up, but I promised myself not to be so available after first dates anymore. As nice as my time with Milo was, I had reservations about what could truly manifest from this relationship, or any relationship for that matter.

"Okay, then. Let's get you out of here. I'll grab the bill. You go." Milo stood up, gently grabbed my face, and leaned over to kiss my forehead. For a day date, it was the perfect kiss.

"Thank you!" I shouted before running off. My slight buzz eased my anxiety about being late but didn't stop me from rushing.

A block away, I saw Lola's rooftop overflowing with people, and a crowd formed outside the door. Inside, the bar was more packed than I'd ever seen. Afraid Sisi would scold me for being late, I tried to sneak in with the crowd. But, of course, she spotted me right away.

"Kay, you're here!" her tone surprisingly fun-spirited.

"It's not even four! What the heck is going on here?" I asked.

"Um, hello! Have you been outside? It's freakin' gorge. And it's a Friday!" Today was unusually warm for early May, and the sun was out without a cloud in the sky. On days like these, New Yorkers flocked to any rooftop they could find.

"I'm surprised you're not more stressed," I told her.

"I was either gonna have a stroke or a shot. So, your girl is feeling good!" I laughed, glad to see Sisi embracing the environment. "Now, do me a favor. Get your butt behind the bar. You're late, and they need you."

"Ah, there's the Sisi I know!"

I followed her order and "busted my butt" behind the bar, where drinks flowed, cash and credit cards flung, and red, green, and white confetti fell from everywhere. I'd never attended a Cinco de Mayo party before but imagined this had to be one of the wildest.

By the end of the night, my hands felt frozen from fetching so many Corona bottles on ice, and I was covered in Modelo from the tap. I knew the tips would be unbelievable, but something else was on my mind. I kept thinking about Milo. Although I promised I wouldn't get ahead of myself, I couldn't resist sending him a text. I sent a photo of the party's aftermath, told him I almost put on a sombrero, and, most importantly, that I had a nice time with him. He responded immediately.

Milo: I had a nice time too.

Pretty in Pink

———

Without a sip of alcohol the night before, I somehow felt hungover the next day. My back ached from bending over the bar, and my knees hurt from standing so long. Even worse, my ankles looked swollen.

I wanted to stay in my cotton sheets, the fresh air from my open window flowing over me. I smiled, knowing I was eight hundred dollars wealthier today. *Kind of makes the pain worth it.*

I picked up my phone from my nightstand—a barrage of notifications, but one stuck out distinctly.

> **Sisi:** What time do you want to meet at Pink House?

Ah, that's right! What time is it? Shit. I got up and showered right away.

———

Pink House was a café downtown and the inspiration behind Brunch in a Bottle's Pink Party. Apparently, Myra came here last year and loved the decor and clientele. It served as an intentionally idyllic Instagram story, more snappable than functional. The pink walls were too bright, the rosy pink tables too tiny, and the baby pink chairs uncomfortable. But I'd hand it to them, the place lived up to its reputation—overly pink.

I also noticed it was overly crowded, comprised mostly of college students and twenty-somethings on their phones or taking photos.

Sisi arrived before me, seated over a muffin and a teeny pink mug. "What is wrong with New York? Either everything is too much or not enough. I'm going to need more coffee than this!" Sisi pointed to her tiny cup when I approached the table. I was about to sit down when someone's shoulder hit my backside.

"Sorry!" he said before hurrying off to his table to jump in his friend's photo. Sisi rolled her eyes.

"Tell me again, why are we here?" she joked. We collided another small table with ours in hopes it'd create enough space for our four teeny coffees, then spent the next hour catching up.

We could have chatted for another few hours, but we both had work to do. I needed to conduct research for Brunch in a Bottle, and Sisi needed to prepare for her nearing meeting with Lola's investor group.

"What about Brunchless?" I asked Sisi about an hour into our work session. "I need to have at least one good idea before my meeting with Samantha next week."

"That makes no sense," Sisi said matter-of-factly.

"More to Brunch? Uh, no, that's terrible."

"Brunchies. Call them Brunchies. Kind of like munchies," she said effortlessly as her gel nails clicked against her laptop's keyboard.

"Yes! That's it! Brunchies!"

"Yeah, yeah, pay me in royalties later." Unfazed, she continued typing.

Having, hopefully, discovered Brunch in a Bottle's new name, I rewarded myself with a break. I slid out of my seat and toward the bathroom when I saw a familiar face walk into Pink House. It was Noah, the tall, messy blond-haired investor from Lola's, whom I dated for a brief time last year. Though our chemistry was undeniable—Noah had a zest for life and the affluence to afford it—his work schedule and short attention span were impossible to keep up with, even if his playfulness and lovable demeanor were hard to resist.

It'd been months since I last saw him. My chest pounded, and my stomach dropped. Unsure of what to do, I scurried inside the bathroom, locked the door, and put my hand on my chest, where I felt my heart beat a mile a minute. *Calm down. You're acting like a lunatic!*

I took a few deep breaths, peed, and stared at myself in the mirror before I heard a knock on the door.

"Hello!" When I didn't respond, the person pressed on. "Let me know if you're doing number two. I'll go somewhere else!" As if I couldn't be any more panicked, I opened the door to find the same guy who bumped into me earlier.

"All yours." I snickered.

I looked around to find Noah before he saw me. There he was, sitting with Sisi at our makeshift table. *Why would she invite him here?*

I couldn't stare from afar forever, so with my nerves somewhat subsided, I tucked my auburn hair back and walked over. If I could speak up to Samantha, then surely, I could face a *kind of* ex.

Noah looked like an actor. He had the best skin, a perfect hairline, and well-fitted clothes. He echoed money and success the moment you saw him. I remembered why I felt so attracted to him.

"Woah, woah, woah. You didn't tell me Kay was here," he said to Sisi. He looked up at me. His jawline was as strong as I remembered. I most certainly blushed but didn't let that prevent my confidence.

"And Sisi, you didn't tell me Noah would be here." I widened my eyes at Sisi to indicate, *What the hell?*

"Oh, give up the act, you two. I had no idea Noah would be here, either. By the way, what the hell are you doing at this place?"

"I have a five percent stake in *this place*. And their coffee isn't half bad." Noah held up his cup.

He was the one investor Sisi had a causal work relationship with. Could be that he is the youngest, and his playful personality diminished any sense of superiority. Noah was in his late twenties, and while immature for his age in some respects, he had an admiration for the finer things, like expensive clothes, global cuisines, and, apparently, small coffees from Pink House.

"The coffee? Isn't it a little tiny?" Sisi asked sarcastically.

"Be careful, you." Noah tilted his head and lifted his eyebrows. "I'll be at that meeting next month, and I'm pretty sure your career is on the agenda."

"Oh please, you know I'm the best thing that ever happened to Lola's." Sisi waved her finger at Noah, continuing their banter while I stood standing, fading into the background.

"Noah! Americano with Soy!" the barista shouted.

"That's me. Kay, why don't you take your seat back?" He stood up and pulled out the tiny pink chair for me. "Sisi, I'll be by Lola's soon. Let's talk about that meeting. I want to help." That was the thing about Noah—he had an irresistible likability about him. He could draw anyone in.

—

I sat down and reopened my laptop without a word to Sisi.

"Kay, I didn't know he'd be here."

"No, I believe you, I believe you. I just wasn't expecting that."

"Well, you look beautiful today!" Sisi tried comforting me, because she knew I would've done anything to lock things in with Noah a year ago.

Yet today was different. I wouldn't let Noah's kindness outshine any confusion he'd put me through before. No. Today I had bigger things to worry about, like getting Samantha to sign off on *Brunchies*.

Simply

Vibrant as ever, Samantha made a grand entrance into LaToulle. Wearing a canary yellow top, teal blue pants, and hot pink heels, I imagined she was conveying some kind of message. Maybe a new coconut rum client? I wasn't sure.

"Team, I have some news," she announced to the floor. "I will be on vacation from the end of May through July."

What? Samantha had already been out of the office more often than usual, relying heavily on her team, but to leave for more than two months was wild. Why was I required to be *on* until six every day, but she could be out as she pleased? CEO or not, I found it sanctimonious.

"I know, I know," she continued. "You'll miss me dearly. But not to worry. I will have check-ins with you in the mornings, and we'll continue our brainstorming meeting virtually."

Rumors came out after that Samantha was recently proposed to and would celebrate the engagement with family in Peru before bringing her daughter to Ibiza for social media content. It wasn't unusual for an executive to take time off in the summer, but the length of her break was longer than anything I'd heard of. I guess the silver lining is that I'd be more available for Lola's with Samantha in a separate time zone.

As was becoming a pattern during Monday meetings, my nerves subsided. I gave an update on my visit to Pink House along with initial ideas for rebranding *Brunch in a Bottle* to *Brunchies.*

"The clientele at Pink House are young and fun, yet sober. They yearn for individuality, which creates uniformity. Like how their individual decision *not* to drink means they're collectively sober. With this in mind, each can should come with their own nonalcoholic personality." As my confidence ensued, I saw Samantha on her phone, hardly paying attention.

"A 'Peachini' for the peach Bellini, a 'Miss Mosa' for the mimosas, and a 'Hail Mary' instead of the spicy Bloody Mary. And we need to drop Brunch in a Bottle. For one, they're not bottles. And for two, it's not catchy. I propose we pitch their new name as Brunchies." The room nodded in agreement, and Samantha finally looked up.

"Let's change Peachini to Peach-a-lini. Otherwise, this looks good." She looked back at her phone.

"Thank you. Should I share it with Myra?"

"Yes, yes, that works. I'll dial in." I wasn't sure why she was so aloof, but I quickly shook it off when I realized I'd be leading my second client pitch.

Natasha provided her update next, which was typical of the ones she'd given before, just with more event work. We hadn't talked much since the Henry's event, so I grabbed her after the meeting to check-in.

"Natasha, that's fun you're working on more events."

"Mm, yeah," she responded. I figured it'd take more than a friendly comment to get through to her.

"Cool... So do you want to grab a coffee later today? I'd love to hear more about it." I discerned my desperation as the words came out of my mouth.

"Um, I can't today."

"What about later this week?" I pressed, despite her hesitation.

"Uh, yeah, sure. Grab me Thursday. My calendar is pretty light."

"That's when Samantha leaves, right?" I asked.

"Yeah, she leaves that morning."

"Perfect, so let's go out after that!" I set up a calendar date with Natasha for Thursday, emailed Myra to meet on Friday, and asked Milo if we could have our next date this weekend. Everyone agreed except Milo.

> **Milo:** Can't wait until the weekend. Meet me at the High Line Wednesday? On your time, any time. I'd love to see you.

Samantha had a weekly doctor's appointment on Wednesdays at 2:00 p.m. *How could I not agree?*

> **Kay:** Okay, you have me for an hour at 2 p.m. Wednesday, 14th Street entrance.

I loved that Milo willingly flexed to my schedule so I didn't have to try and fit into his. And I was excited to explore where this flirtation could go. We had a chemistry, but romantic chemistry? I wasn't sure yet. I just knew I wanted to find out.

Sweet and Sugared

The overcast sky made for a cooler spring day. Perfect for meeting Milo at the High Line, an old subway line turned into an outdoor walking path in downtown Manhattan. It cut through beautiful high rises and greenery.

I knew I had a crush on Milo because I put extra effort into my outfit today. I even bought a new bomber jacket last night for today's date. It paired well with my dark green cargo pants and white, low-rise sneakers. Not that I felt pressure to look any type of way with Milo, but I fed into his streetwear style, and he noticed.

"You look nice," he greeted me before leaning in for a hug. "Remind me. How long do I have you for?" He took my hand and led me up the stairs to the High Line.

"An hour. No more, no less," I teased.

"Dang, I was hoping you'd change your mind and I'd have you longer." I should have realized Milo asked me here because of the architecture. I assumed he wanted to share his knowledge about the buildings and hotel designs, especially after I showed interest in the subject on our previous date. And he was right. I enjoyed learning about his work. Almost as much as I enjoyed the people watching. A combination of local New Yorkers and tourists—with a more sophisticated taste for exploring the city beyond typical areas like Rockefeller Center and Time Square—strolled along the walkway.

Milo pointed to several buildings we passed to tell me about their history and design concepts. Each time he leaned in, the smell of his cologne was as sexy as the strength of his arm muscle against mine. Surrounded by dozens of people, I somehow felt alone with him, and I wanted more.

"I could really use a pick me up before heading back to the office," I said after we passed a coffee stand about thirty minutes into our walk.

"Long night ahead?"

"Uh, yeah. But once Samantha leaves, I'll have more time to myself."

"Well, let's get you caffeinated then. I won't keep you too much longer." It began raining as we waited in line. "Ah, está chispeando," Milo muttered in Spanish. It was the first time I heard him speak it.

"Huh?" I asked.

"Ah, I said it's drizzling. This weather reminds me of Miami."

"You lived in Miami?"

"Yup. Before New York and after Spain."

"Ah, so you were a party boy?" I joked, trying to glean more into Milo's past.

"Ha, just a little bit. I actually went to the University of Miami for undergrad. My English wasn't great at the time, so I moved somewhere that wouldn't be a problem. I just hated how rain would come out of nowhere. Kind of like this." We looked up at the sky and then down the walkway. People began dashing for cover, the rain growing more intense.

"Well, this isn't Miami, but it looks like it's about to downpour!" I said. In seconds, the drizzle turned into heavy rain.

Milo took off his jacket and swung it over our heads. He led us inside Chelsea Market, an oversized shopping center in the Meatpacking District with various cafés, eateries, and stores. Inside, he shook out his wet coat, took my hand, and navigated us through a packed corridor of people to a small bakery.

"Let me guess. You helped build something in here too?" I asked, wondering how he knew how to get around.

"Actually, no. I just smelled something really good." I laughed because he was totally serious. It smelled like freshly baked bread and sugary cupcakes.

A crowd of people must have had the same idea because they amassed around us as we incidentally stood in the bakery's line. Elbows bumped us from left and right, so Milo stood behind me and placed his arms over mine to mitigate the blows. I felt his chest against my back and gave into an urge I could no longer resist.

I turned around and kissed him, my lips against his face, a bit wet from the rain. He pulled away to look at me, his eyes opened in shock, his mouth with a slight grin. Without another word, we kissed again. Slowly, passionately. Again, I could have sworn we were the only two in the room.

"Hey, you two gonna order or what?" a grumpy man yelled at us from behind.

"Geez, get a room!" another murmured under her breath. We stepped up to the counter. Ruffled, I ordered a flat white, and Milo ordered a coffee with cream.

"I got it," I said, wanting to repay him for our first date. I also had the extra cash to spend more easily these days. We moved to the second counter and waited for our drinks. I felt the tension between us like I wanted to kiss him again. He must have read my mind because he looked at me and leaned in.

For the first time in my life, I was one of two people, in public, who absolutely "needed to get a room."

Back at the office, I wasn't sure how I'd get the butterflies out of my belly or the smile off my face. Today proved that Milo was, most definitely, not in the friend zone. At my desk, I took a deep breath and sent him a message,

> **Kay:** I made it back. Thank you for show-
> ing me another side of the High Line I
> hadn't seen before.

> **Milo:** Thanks for showing me another side
> of you I hadn't seen before.

His instant reply gave me goosebumps. I looked around to see if anyone saw me grinning at my phone screen. Contrary, my colleagues had their heads down working. I assumed all for the same reason—Samantha was leaving tomorrow, and there was a lot to do beforehand. *Suppose I should join them.*

A few hours later and an expensed late-night takeout meal to the office, I finished preparing for my meeting with Myra. I planned to scan over my inbox one last time when I saw Natasha walking toward our desks. She had a bottle of wine and two glasses.

"Please tell me you're up for a drink," she said. I was surprised to see her initiate such an amicable gesture.

"I was just about to leave, but why not?" This was surely a better way to crack Natasha than a coffee date tomorrow afternoon.

She poured a glass of South African Chenin Blanc, a bottle from the office collection. Samantha often received beverages as gifts, so many that she ordered a separate wine cooler for the staff.

"Cheers!" Natasha toasted my glass.

"Cheers," I conceded.

The office had nearly all but cleared out as we sat adjacent to one another—me at my desk and Natasha at Andre's. For once, he actually left on time.

"So, what are you working on before you leave?" she asked. In an attempt to form a friendship, I showed her the Brunchies campaign. "Hm, not too bad," she said, looking over my pitch.

A drink later and I knew more about Natasha than I ever thought I would. To my surprise, she wasn't as enthusiastic about LaToulle as she let on. "Honestly, I just want to move back to Canada and forget about this place. I'm only here to show my parents I'm as great as Bri, but they're not convinced."

"So you don't want to stay at LaToulle?" I figured now was as good a time as ever to get her angle on the client lead role.

"*Want*? I have no choice," she said.

"What do you mean?"

"I'm here on a work visa. If I don't stay at LaToulle, I'm almost certainly going home."

"Kind of sounds like what you want, right?"

"Uh, does anyone really know what they want?" Natasha took another sip of her wine. She was clearly a lightweight and definitely confused. I thought it best not to press her further, but she continued on freely. "I mean, I could stay here and go after a better role. I did talk to Samantha about that."

"Wait, really?" I couldn't believe she'd talked with Samantha about her trajectory before I did.

"See, this is why I don't drink. I get tipsy too fast and say too much."

"No, no, it's okay. That's great for you!" I put on a warm smile that felt cold inside.

"I guess so. Hard to know what she was thinking, though. You must be eyeing that client lead role, right?"

"Um, I hadn't really thought about it." I lied through my teeth but didn't want to give away that I'd not been savvy enough to talk to Samantha yet.

"Mm."

We finished our drinks, walked out together, and jumped on our respective trains home. *Is this what it was like to have a frenemy?*

Make It a Double

My meeting with Myra was top of mind this morning as I prepared to pitch my idea for rebranding *Brunch in a Bottle* to *Brunchies*.

My outfit resembled the office. I wore a white blazer, white pants, and just a dash of color—my royal blue heels. It was a bold choice I hoped would help exude the confidence I was starting to build. *You got this*, I told myself on the way to the meeting.

At the start of the video call, only myself, Myra, and one of Myra's associates were on. No Samantha. We waited a couple of minutes and through some awkward silence when I had a feeling Samantha wouldn't join. It wasn't like her to ever be late.

"Sorry to keep you waiting, Myra. Let me ping her again," I said.

> **Kay:** I'm on the Zoom with Myra. Do you need the meeting ID?

"Should only be a moment," I reassured Myra, who over video wore a blank expression.

Samantha: Can't make it today. You got it.
Send me an update later.

Her text sent a lump through my throat.

"My apologies, but Samantha can't make it. If you're willing, I'd love to walk through our pitch without her." I searched for Myra's reaction through the camera. She looked disappointed but assented.

Over the next ten minutes, I recited the pitch I gave Samantha a few days earlier, only this time with her recommended tweaks. I emphasized the legacy of LaToulle, including the type of clients we typically worked with but that, like the broader culture, we were evolving too.

"Trends clearly show those turning the legal drinking age are, in fact, not drinking. They're going so far as to label binge drinking 'cheugy,' a term coined against millennials to *describe someone who is out of date or trying too hard.*"

Myra laughed. "Oh yes. We know what cheugy means. It's what we're trying to avoid." Her approval gave me relief, so I moved on to the name reveal.

"I'm glad you agree because, with this vision in mind, we also believe Brunch in a Bottle would be better received if it wasn't called, well, Brunch in a Bottle." Though Myra had been commendatory thus far, suggesting a name change was a big deal.

"Brunchies," I announced and screen shared a suggested logo. "And each flavor has a fun twist, like Peach-a-lini, Miss Mosa, and Hail Mary," I continued, animating each can on the shared screen. I paused for her reaction, but Myra remained quiet. Looking away from the camera, her expression took a one-eighty. As I wavered on what to say next, the conference room door swung open.

"Kay! Samantha can't make your meeting with brunch something." It was Andre, a little too late and a lot too inappropriate. "Oh, sorry, ladies. I see you've already started." He pursed his lips and tiptoed out of the room, as if it'd erase what he'd just done.

I had a few options—go cold and fumble the call; run out of the room and pretend I never met Myra; or continue on, knowing Andre's words spoke for him. Not me.

I chose the latter. "Myra, what are you thinking?" I finally asked.

"I'm not sure." I didn't understand why she wouldn't tell me.

"What about it don't you love?" I stuck to the content. I didn't let her concern deter me.

"Well, the whole *Brunchies* thing. It will be a lot of work for us to rebrand the cans... and the names. Aren't they a bit cheesy?"

Shit. My heart dropped, and my head wanted to too. But I wore a smile and remained present as our conversation unfolded.

"I hear you. This is the first go at it. How about we come back with a few more ideas, and—"

"As I said, I don't love it. But I could be proven wrong. I have no idea about the market in New York. I'm an Austin girl, born and raised." She gave me an inch. How could I take a mile?

"Why don't we try a proof of concept? Beta test the rebrand in New York. We know the market here and restaurants that could help promote it." Myra nodded.

"Okay, okay." I could tell she was ruminating on the idea. "Okay," she said a third time. "Let's do this. I'll speak with the manufacturer. They should be able to implement the new logo in a couple of weeks." Myra talked over logistics, her associate taking notes, then we settled on a date.

"Fourth of July it is! We'll host a launch party you won't forget. I even have the perfect venue in mind." Because this time, I did. A wave of optimism rushed over me. I couldn't wait to share the news with Samantha.

Pinot Noir

——

Sisi: Take the night off. I'm all set! But let's do after-work drinks tomorrow?

Kay: Yes! Also, I can help with any extra shifts you need covered. My body is finally adjusting to bartending again.

Fast cash is instantaneously rewarding, and I'd become accustomed to the extra buffer each week. I especially loved indulging in takeout lattes and lunch and wasn't willing to give it up anytime soon.

Sisi: Of course. Can you work Sunday brunches?

Kay: Perfect!

It wasn't lost on me how lucky I was to curate the schedule of my second job, especially with Samantha away. But considering I had this night off, I asked Milo if he wanted to see me, so long as it involved ordering in and bad TV.

> **Milo:** I've been working too much. This
> sounds perfect.

Knowing Milo was coming over got me excited, especially because he'd be the first guy to visit my studio apartment.

—

"You're a busy lady, huh?" Milo joked. He arrived at my apartment before me.

"Sorry! Subway trouble!"

"I hope you like red." He lifted a bottle of wine in one hand and gave me a half-hug with the other. He wore fitted tan pants, a zip up hoodie, and the familiar pair of Vans. His smile revealed one dimple, only slightly concealed by his facial scruff.

"I do! Thank you! And I hope you like pad Thai," I said.

"Love it!"

Inside, he asked about my day right away. "Wait, you're not going to let me change into comfy clothes first?"

"No! I want to hear all about your call. Plus, you look great in that suit." Smitten with his compliment, I kicked off my heels, the comfort of which made me want to rip off my bra too. But I was a lady, and I'd wait.

"I need a drink, you?" In my white suit, I poured red wine for us both.

"Doesn't seem like I have a choice," he said in jest before I passed him a glass. I sat on the couch across from Milo, my legs crossed. While telling him about my day, I threw my hair up in a loose bun, said *like* too many times, and accidentally swallowed too large a gulp of wine that I coughed. Milo was unfazed. With our romantic chemistry proclaimed at the High Line, I sat with him unworried about being me.

"So why wouldn't Samantha join the call?" Milo asked.

"Ya know, I'm still not sure, but thinking more about it, she hardly interacts with clients aside from mingling at cocktail parties and schmoozing them on initial pitches. I mean, she's been out of the office more than she's been in it this year."

"Do you think she just knows you can handle it for her?" Milo suggested.

"Yeah, maybe. I just always thought I'd learn more from her when it came to clients. But she left me on my own with this one." I shrugged and took another sip of wine.

"Sounds like you're more than capable on your own, but if you want a mentor, it doesn't sound like you'll get it from that place."

"I want a promotion! I love the client work but want to be paid for it. Our promotion cycle is, like, a month away. If I don't get it, I'll be so disappointed." As the words came out of my mouth, I realized just how badly I wanted it and how much pressure I felt to earn it.

"There's no reason why you shouldn't get it. But make sure they give you what you're worth. In my last job, my boss took advantage of my work ethic. Dangled small bonuses in front of me, which kept me much longer than it should've. I'm just glad I finally started working for myself."

"What do you mean by your last job?"

"In Miami before I came here for grad school." Milo told me how he'd managed large teams and multimillion-dollar projects. "There was a lot of pressure, and I kept thinking I'd get a bigger salary, a better title, but it never came."

"But look at you now! You've got your own business!"

"Yeah, but it's not always so great. When I'm out of school, I'll get my own staff, and they can deal with the hands-on stuff." He laughed and took a sip. "I mean, it's fine."

"Everyone knows fine is not fine," I said to him.

"Yeah, but it's only while I'm in school because it's flexible." While Milo shared his aspirations to grow his business, I got a notification the food delivery would be late.

"So what's the plan then? You said a movie?" he asked.

"Yes! Let's pick one." I moved closer to him on my double-cushioned sofa. We looked at each other, smiling, like two kids afraid to reveal they had a crush on one another. His dark brown eyes and boyish smirk made me want to kiss him, but I resisted my urge.

Scrolling through Netflix, Milo wasn't convinced when I suggested several of this year's Oscar-nominated films. Instead, he suggested classic movies like *Fight Club* or *Pulp Fiction*.

"We're going to spend more time picking out a movie than watching one," I half-joked, half-complained. Milo continued flicking through options when, after twenty minutes of indecision, my phone rang. The food finally arrived. "You're lucky," I joked before retrieving our Thai order.

"Let me get it for us," Milo insisted.

"No, no, it's fine. I have the key!" I said, dangling it in my hand. "Plus, I need you to watch more trailers and expand your movie horizons!"

When I came back, Milo got up to help. He grabbed the noodle dish I was struggling to hold, touching my hand as we set it on the table. "Wow, be careful!"

But it was too late. It was like our touch was the catalyst he needed to initiate what I desired on the couch. Forget his taste in movies. This was hot. He pulled me toward him in a quick swoop, taking the next dish out of my hand and placing it on the table behind me. We were face-to-face now.

"Are we not going to eat?" I asked playfully.

He shook his head from side to side. "Not yet." His look made me feel wanted and craved, like I was the most desirable girl in his world. I grabbed his arms, and he ripped off my blazer, pulling down my tank top and bra to reveal the right side of my chest. He kissed me there before taking it all off.

I pulled his shirt over his head and grasped his arms and back as he carried me to the couch. I took my pants off and unbuttoned his before I sat on top of him. We moved in rhythm. He held me like he adored me. After we both came, we lay together, quiet and comfortable.

"I guess dessert came before dinner," Milo broke our silence. He caressed my hair before we ultimately dug into dinner. Then we cuddled while watching one of the movies he picked out.

"Kay, I want you to be my girlfriend," he whispered before we fell asleep. In my silence, I hoped he knew I could feel the same, if not just yet.

The next morning, we didn't talk about the girlfriend comment. Instead, Milo went down on me before showering and leaving for one of his jobs in Midtown. Shortly after, I headed to Lola's, arriving a little early to meet Sisi.

"Sisi!" I found her in her office.

"Ah!" She jumped out of her seat. "Are you trying to give me a damn heart attack?" She swiveled her chair around and placed her hand over her heart.

"Sorry, I didn't mean to scare you!" I tried not to laugh.

"Uh, no, it's okay." She adjusted her extensions in her bedazzled mirror. "What are you doing here so early?" she asked. I immediately spilled about my night with Milo. "Ah! This is amazing. I love that guy."

"He's not so bad. But it's moving so easily, I'm worried. Like something's gotta go wrong."

"Oh, relax, you're just used to guys breadcrumbing you. It's about time you meet someone different."

"Mm, I think he wants me to be his girlfriend..."

"What do you mean *think*?"

"Well, he told me last night, but I didn't say anything."

"Why? That is so weird," Sisi said with an attitude. I gave her a look like, *I know. That's why I'm telling you all this.*

"Okay, okay. Why don't you just take a beat? Hey! Don't touch those." I turned around to see Sisi was distracted by one of the cocktail waitresses. "We're tossing out those old shirts. The new black shirts are over there." She pointed to another box. "Grab a small for the new girl. Thanks, love." She turned her attention back to me. "Ugh, sorry. We've been hiring like crazy, and I have too many black outfits lying around. The old ones were so—"

"Awful."

"Seriously! The cut was too low even for *my* boobs."

"Ha, yes! And the cotton felt like sandpaper," I added.

"Okay, anyway, I was saying. If I were you, I would tell Milo you want to enjoy getting to know him before you throw a label on it."

"Totally. I mean... I'm not dating for the sake of dating anymore."

"Just be happy you met someone you *can* date. I had a third date this week. You know the guy I thought was on steroids? He called me Sally. Sally! I've met the guy, like, three times, and he still didn't know my name!"

"Woah, seriously? He was hot, though." I attempted to make her feel better.

"Yeah, he was, huh? But anyway, I'm trying to say Milo knows what he wants. Summer is here, and your boss is away.

Let's have fun this next month. We'll be together more, and there are enough messes to clean up around here as is. We don't need to get ourselves into any more."

Touché, Si. Touché.

Red Blend

———

Like a red wine and chocolate torte, Milo and I paired wonderfully. Dating over the next few weeks, I experienced just how compatible we were. Like the way our busy work schedules mirrored one other and the appreciation we shared for slivers of personal time in between. Or our love for the aroma of freshly brewed coffee in the morning and decadent meals in the evening after a long day. Everything about us had been easy.

We slept over at each other's apartments, already leaving some of our essentials for familiarity and comfort. Sometimes Milo would even arrive at mine before me and I'd come home to him taking over my kitchen. He'd whip up different Latin, Mediterranean, and Middle Eastern dishes—his favorites— always with his shirt off. He'd move from the stove to the kitchen sink and in and out of my fridge. He set the mood with good music, dimmed lights, and a lit candle, each time continuing our routine of dessert before dinner.

When we did eat, he would share the memories he'd experienced through each dish. Like how he and his grandfather would pick up fresh seafood on Sundays to make paella. Or how his aunt made the best mantecados every Christmas. And when he didn't cook Spanish foods, he'd tell me where and how he learned about other cuisines. Like how a past coworker from Morocco brought him to a tajine restaurant, and Milo learned how to cook with one the next day.

The best part about being with him is that we laughed. Boy, did we laugh, sharing similar humor despite coming from different places. And I loved listening to his dreams and aspirations. Milo was the first guy I met who shared his vision of success with me. Each morning with him, I awoke a little love stoned. It was the best nonrelationship relationship I'd been in. This is why when Milo asked me again if I was ready to be his girlfriend, I told him not yet.

--

At LaToulle, I'd taken the past few weeks to dim my creativity and relieve some stress. I'd been waiting on some deliverables from clients and knew Samantha was in la-la land, so I decided now was a good time to ease any pressure I typically put on myself. That was, until today.

"Kay, did you see the email from Samantha?" Andre asked when I walked into the office. I was sweating from the June heat.

"Not yet. I haven't checked my phone all morning." This was true because I'd been sitting in bed with Milo while we sipped coffee and talked about our favorite desserts. Mine were macaroons, and his were Snicker bars.

Andre grimaced. "Uh, you're not going to like what she has to say." Few things are worse than getting a clue to bad news without the bad news itself. I opened my laptop immediately and saw her email.

Samantha: Kay, can you forward me that plan for your little Brunchies event? I need

to show the board. Also, I won't be back in
town for it. I trust you'll tell Myra.

My jaw dropped. Everything about her message irked
me. "My little event," as if insignificant. "I need to show the
board," as if she'd given input. And "tell Myra," as if I was
the one who'd be out of town.

"Oh, sweetie, you'll be fine. Those cans are tacky anyway,"
Andre said after he saw I read her message.

"Those cans are a potential account, one I've worked really
hard to land," I said in a moment of severe irritation.

"So, what are you going to do, tell Samantha? Good luck
with that, darling." Andre reeked of snark. That and I realized
just how much of a puppet he was to her. The worst part—he
was right. There was nothing I could say because Samantha
left no room for dissent.

Natasha must have smelled conflict because she returned
to our desks. "What's going on?" she asked.

"Well, if it isn't miss snoopy herself," Andre said.

"Oh please, as if I don't know this is about Samantha.
What? She's blowing you off too?" Natasha asked, seemingly
frustrated with Samantha as well. I showed her the email,
continuing my new approach at winning her over.

"Guess Brunchies isn't such a big deal after all," she said.

"Are neither of you two going to support me here?" I asked,
unable to hide my irritation any longer.

"Well, when I try to find you, you're usually not here,"
Natasha snapped back. I knew she was referring to my leaving
around five o'clock most days.

"Well, guess it doesn't serve me to stay here all night anyway," I said.

"Girl, be careful. If others get a whiff of that attitude..." Andre said, waving his hand in front of his nose. "All I'm saying is you don't want to jeopardize that promotion."

"So where have you been, anyway?" Natasha followed up, surprisingly ignoring Andre's promotion comment. Maybe she'd finally come to terms that I was favored for it.

"What do you mean? I'm right here," I asked.

"I notice you've been leaving, like, on time every day, which no one ever does. Are you just taking a break now that Samantha's not here?"

"She's probably dating someone," Andre chimed in.

"Yeah, maybe something like that," I conceded. Better they assume my love life was the distraction opposed to my second job. But their words also struck me. *"Dating."* Milo and I were indeed dating, but how long would that be enough?

Another Round

Given Samantha's aloofness around my "little Brunchies event," I took advantage of my situation. I preferred my routine evening plans over extra time at the office, despite Natasha's predictable side-eye whenever I left on time. To me, it was worth it—more cash tips; more time with Milo.

Every night I spent with him, the more intimate we grew. One evening I told him about my childhood dream of living in New York. Growing up in a small town, I'd cut out fashion magazines and paste them along my bedroom walls for inspiration to make it one day, like the girls in the photo.

Another time, he shared his inspiration to move to the US, and his favorite professor steered him to pursue architecture. Then one day, he aspired to own his own firm because he loved making clients happy and thought he had the training and interpersonal skills to do it.

We both shared a similar drive to be something more than our circumstances assumed because we both weren't fed from a silver spoon. But with each intimate moment and evening together, we were cementing our fate. And, well, cement is hard to break. I wondered if we were ready to be grounded?

"Every time I hear about you two, there's nothing wrong!" Sisi said, fed up with my doubts about mine and Milo's budding relationship. It'd been over a month since our first date.

"When we're together, we're great, but when we're apart, I wonder what I want out of this. I don't know. I guess I just overthink it," I told her.

"What's the problem?" Sisi asked, genuinely confused. I realized I was too.

"You're right. There isn't one. I like Milo a lot. I just think about, you know, how we ran into Noah, for instance. It's like I'd rather torture myself wanting someone I can't have than appreciate the person I do." As the words left my mouth, guilt submerged me.

"Are you just not into him?" It was a fair question, but that wasn't it.

"No, it's so not that. I love our time together. It's just, just…" my voice trailed.

"You're bored," Sisi stated as if a matter of fact.

"I'm not bored! It's like good just isn't good enough. Like if he and I get serious, what else might I be missing?" I huffed, frustrated by my inability to better define how I felt.

"Well, whatever you do, I wouldn't idealize Noah. Love the guy, but he was a pariah to your sanity." Sisi had no problem reminding me of Noah's ways. It's true. He is a fun-loving, attractive guy but much better suited as a friend or, in my case, as an acquaintance.

I only wished our circumstances had led us down the friend path. Instead, when I was introduced to Noah as Lola's newest investor last year, it was clear he had an infatuation with me. Of course, I reciprocated, and we intertwined immediately. But our whimsical fling ended when he admitted he'd found "the girl of his dreams" a few months later. She lasted a couple of more months, and then another came along.

"Anyway, Kay, life isn't a Tetris board—you don't need it all to fit perfectly," Sisi said. She picked up a stack of papers and began reviewing them.

"Since when do you play Tetris?" I asked, hoping to end this conversation. If not to end my self-sabotage, then for Sisi's sanity.

"Uh, I don't. It's on my mind from one of my interviews today. One guy wrote on here that he's a high scorer on his Tetris app." She showed me his résumé. "So weird!"

"These are bartenders?"

"No, I need a new manager!" I looked at her like, *Are you firing me?* "You're great, Kay, but I should reframe. I need a new *general manager*. I met with the investor group. Not only are you looking at Lola's newest investor, but they're also making me the head of operations!" She opened her mouth, no longer able to contain her excitement.

"No way! Sisi, that is... wow. That is amazing! From waitress to investor and head of operations!" I shook my head in astonishment. Sisi was too ingrained in the success of the business to continue managing the day-to-day schedules and BS that went with it, so her new role made sense. It was just incredible what she'd been able to accomplish here.

"I know, right? But it won't happen for another couple of months. I need to hire someone, get them up to speed, yada yada. Hey, remind me," she changed the subject, "you'll be here for brunch Sunday, right?" I nodded, knowing she didn't want to spend any more time celebrating herself.

"So, as the official new head of operations, can you help me out with something?" I asked.

"Uh oh. What?"

"I need a place for my Brunchies event. I thought we could do it here. The rooftop?"

"Hmm... depends when. We're totally booked this month."

"Fourth of July?" I asked nervously, knowing New York City bars didn't yield visitors on this day. Everyone was too busy at their summer homes or flooding the streets to see the fireworks. "I already have a guest list! Worst case, there will at least be *some* people here. Please!"

"Um... Ya know what? Yeah, sure. I like it! We'll give whoever's stuck in the city a place to go."

"Ah! Thank you! This is why you're the new head of operations." I gave her an obnoxious wink.

"Yeah, don't do that." I had to laugh at how uncomfortable she became. Also, if I didn't laugh, I'd likely cry. Working at Lola's helped my career as much as it prolonged it, so I hoped my two worlds could collide without consequence.

That Saturday evening, the weather made for a beautiful Lola's rooftop. Perfect for me, as I worked inside on the downstairs floor, using the quiet time to brainstorm about Brunchies. We were ten days out from the event, and because they weren't already our client, I wanted to go above and beyond to ensure they would be. I scribbled on receipt paper, sketching out ideas. *That promotion could and would be mine.*

Deep in brainstorming mode, I heard Sisi's voice rise. "Milo! You're such a sweetheart." She greeted him at the door before they both walked over to me at the bar. "You're a lucky girl, Kay! I wish someone showed up with goodies for me!"

Blushing, Milo handed me a little baggy with a Magnolia's Bakery logo. "I picked you up something. I think you mentioned it's your favorite." I opened the baggy to find macaroons.

"Aw, Milo. This is so sweet!" His face lit up when I took a bite of one. "Hey, I thought you were working?" I asked, my mouth full of coconut flour.

"I finished a little early because it's about to rain. Actually, I think it's starting now." *What?* This meant any crowd upstairs would be rushing down to avoid the rain at any moment.

"Si!" I yelled. She was now by the host stand organizing stationary.

"Finally! I was hoping you'd share whatever you got there." She whizzed over to grab a macaroon.

"Did you know it's about to rain?" I asked. Sisi was always weather prepared because of how much it impacted the business.

"Ya know what? No!" she said, her mouth now also full of coconut flour. We looked toward the stairs and saw a few people coming in from the rooftop, shielding their heads from the rain. Those few people quickly turned into a stampede of guests hurrying down as rain clanked loudly against the ceiling.

"I'm gonna go check on them upstairs," Sisi said. She headed toward the back stairwell that also led to the roof. I knew she'd help the waitstaff close out bills and keep the computer systems from getting wet. "You good down here?" she asked.

"Um, yeah, I should be all right!" Because I was working alone, I didn't have to split tips. So as overbearing as the crowd may get, it'd be more lucrative to handle it on my own. But as they swarmed, I got overwhelmed. Fortunately, Milo realized this and swung behind the bar to help.

"You know how to bartend?" I asked him.

"Um, I know how to pour things." His response was far from assuring.

"Just follow my lead."

I directed Milo during the rush, showing him the credit card machine, having him hand out beer bottles, and asking him to wipe the bar clean from dripping wet elbows.

The rush must have lasted nearly an hour before things settled down. And when it did, I saw someone in the crowd who made my heart stop and my face flush—the feeling I'd learned to repress before a presentation but hadn't practiced for this. It was Adam.

Spirit

Adam casually stood over one of the high-top tables across the bar, sipping a beer among a small group of people. The moment I spotted him, he looked at me too. I quickly turned away, but it'd be impossible to deny we saw one another, if only my pounding heart to prove it.

I shouldn't be, but I was embarrassed. I didn't want Adam to see me like this—sweaty, unkempt, and dirty from bartending a mad crowd. I wanted to uphold any desirable image he may have of me, even if I hadn't seen the sleazebag in a couple of months.

I felt his gaze continue while Milo helped me bartend. I wondered if he saw Milo place his hand on my hips to squeeze by or the kiss he gave my cheek.

"Kay, I'm running to the bathroom. You're good now, right?"

"Um, oh, yes. Yes, thank you, Milo!" He kissed me again.

Adam must have considered this his window of opportunity, because the next thing I knew, he was at the bar. "I didn't know you worked here." His voice was still as deep and sexy as I remembered.

I didn't know how to respond or if I wanted to. "Mhm," I landed on.

"Who's the guy?"

As if it were his business.

"A friend."

"How have you been?"

"Good, thanks." I couldn't mask my resentment. I was still bitter about how things ended. Fortunately, another customer wanted to pay, so I took a few steps away from Adam to grab her credit card.

After I closed out the check, Adam said the words I would have loved to hear a couple of months ago. "I miss you, and I want to see you again." Before I could reply, Milo reentered the bar.

"Still holding it down?" he asked.

Adam walked away, a sudden reminder he's the kind of person who avoids displeasure. "Was that guy all set?" Milo pointed to Adam, confused he hadn't ordered anything.

"Um, yeah, I guess so." I didn't want Milo to know anything about him. That just a couple of months prior, he was someone who made me stir crazy but whom I wanted to want me nonetheless.

"Mm... you sure?" He likely had a sense our encounter was more loaded than I let on.

"I'm sure. So hey, you did pretty well back here." I changed the subject to shake off the stain of Adam.

"Ha, yeah, thanks," Milo said, peering down at his clothes, which were now wet with beer and juice. "I have an early morning and don't have a change of clothes at your place. Let's meet tomorrow?"

"Definitely. I'll be home after my brunch shift." I kissed him goodbye. "Thank you again. For everything."

He kissed my forehead. "Does this mean you'll be my girlfriend?" He asked what had become a running joke. I just smiled, knowing he probably wouldn't allow it as a response for much longer.

"What a freakin' day, man," Sisi said, grabbing a stool a couple of hours later. We just finished the last call, and I was closing out my checks. "You must have made a killing back here."

"Si, I'm at nearly a thousand dollars. Before tip out, but still." She widened her eyes and dropped her jaw.

"That's wild. Are you going to give some to Milo?"

"Thought about it, but I doubt he'd take anything."

"Yeah, good point," she said, cracking open a beer can.

"I'll ask him to dinner instead."

"Ooh, good idea! Though he'd probably prefer you commit to being his girlfriend instead."

"Hmm, probably." I felt bad thinking about it.

Sisi took a drink of her beer. "Ah! That is the best thing I've had all day."

"I could use one too. Did you see who was here?" I asked. She looked at me like, *No, tell me.* "Adam."

"What? No! I was running around the whole time. I totally missed him. Did he talk to you?"

"Uh, yes." I went on to tell her what had happened.

"You're not thinking of talking to him again, are you?"

"Of course not!"

"Good. Because I won't even hire him back here again as a DJ. Besides, Milo is way better. Look at you when you're with him! You're so yourself!"

"Oh gee, thanks."

"You know what I mean. Now, hand me your cash report. Let's get out of here! I'm beat." As I waited for Sisi to submit my report on her computer and quantify my tip out, I got a text.

Adam: You looked good behind the bar

A very Adam-like text. It said enough without saying much of anything. And though it was a less than ideal way to run into him, I felt validated knowing he wanted to see me again, like our short-lived romance wasn't a total mirage.

"Kay!" Sisi screamed. "You made nine hundred and fifty dollars!"

"Ah, I knew I killed it tonight."

"Well, nine hundred and fifty-eight, to be exact. But damn, girl! You owe me dinner too!" I sure did. Who needed drama for one when I could afford dinner for three?

Muddled

My heart pounded when I received yet another message from him.

Adam: When will I see you again?

I tried my best to shake off the feeling of distress mixed with an undeniable yearning to, in fact, see him again. My better judgment knew I shouldn't, but the attention from someone whom I assumed was out of my league and unattainable, albeit inconsiderate, gave me the urge to.

I turned my attention away from Adam and toward myself. I'd just gotten home from a Sunday brunch shift, and my head ached from the loud music. I took a shower and laid on my couch to get a grip. After a few minutes of staring at the ceiling, I initiated the dinner I believed I owed Milo. I wouldn't let today be the day I went against my better judgment.

Kay: Hey! Let's meet at Barano. It's in your neighborhood and my treat. I owe you from last night.

Milo: You don't owe me anything! But I won't say no to dinner with you.

A few hours later, we met for a lovely Italian meal paired with a bottle of Montepulciano. When we finished our plates, I surprised him with a handful of Snickers in my purse.

"An extra thank you." I smiled.

"Oh, stealing my tricks, huh?"

"Just trying to get you to take me home." I paid the bill, and we walked a few streets to Milo's. He held my hand and pointed out his favorite buildings on the way. Inside his studio, we laid down, spooning while watching TV. When we finally went to bed, Milo continued playing big spoon. He caressed my hair and gently told me, "I love being with you, Kay. You're creative. You're a great listener. You work hard for what you want."

"Keep going," I joked.

"Seriously! I feel so good with you, and I see us accomplishing a lot. Together." I thought I could predict what would come next, that Milo would evaluate our relationship status or tell me he wanted to be my boyfriend, again. My chest tightened, and I became anxious. I'd wanted to meet someone like Milo, someone enchanting and effortless, but now, it all felt too real. I wondered if I was ready.

"Oh, and you're beautiful." He chuckled and kissed the side of my cheek. "Goodnight, Kay."

I repressed the sigh of relief I wanted to exhale. In the dark, Milo couldn't read my facial expressions, and tonight I didn't want him to.

I woke up with more energy than usual and ran through my morning routine, Milo still in bed.

"Have you seen my keys?" I shouted. It was only 7:00 a.m., but I was excited to get to the office and finish planning the

Brunchies event, even if it might be the only work we do with them.

"They're on the table," Milo called out. "Where's my kiss?"

"It's right here." I walked to the bed and bent over to kiss his lips.

"Go get 'em!" Milo slapped my butt before I left. Another thing to love about Milo—he unabashedly supported my work.

On my way to LaToulle's, I committed to ignoring Adam's most recent text and reached out to Olivia instead. I hadn't seen her since the Henry's event and thought now would be a good time to catch up. She'd managed so many promo parties with Bryan, I hoped she'd offer an idea or two to enhance the Brunchies party plans. I just wasn't sure she'd be into it. She'd never helped me with work before—but surprisingly, she responded right away.

Olivia: Love it! Just let me know where, xoxo.

I chose a café near my office of caliber for Olivia—overly priced and dainty. Inside were white bistro tables and floral decorates that matched the porcelain plates of overly decadent brunch food. Olivia, of course, was late.

While waiting, I got a message.

Samantha: Good work on the pitch! Get
time with me tomorrow. Need to talk to you.

I tried dissecting what she meant. *Bad, good? Had I done something wrong?* Before I could harp on her cryptic message for too long, Olivia arrived. She looked different. More radiant, her skin fresher, and her hair… it was chopped up to her ears.

"Liv! Your hair!" I couldn't resist commenting.

"You like the new glow up?" she asked, patting the ends of her symmetric hairline.

"It looks amazing!" And it did. She looked more mature, and her defined cheekbones carried her new cut well.

"I know, right?" She took a seat adjacent to me. We took a few moments to catch up on things, like her recent work project, new manicurist, and how her shorter hair transformed her worldview.

"Are you still seeing Bryan?" I asked, knowing she'd pretend she didn't love talking about him.

"Seeing? Yes. Dating? No. We've decided we're much better at business than romance." *Huh?* "We're promoting together now. I have all the hot friends and connections. He has all the relationships with the liquor brands and venues." Claiming she had "all" the connections was a stretch, but I had to give it to her, she was more focused than before.

"Good for you! I'm happy to hear that."

"You really need to come to the next event. You will *love* it!"

"I actually wanted to talk to you about that," I said before sharing more about Brunchies. Typically, I would expect Olivia to meet this conversation with hesitation or boredom, but to my surprise, she was incredibly attentive. Maybe she was right about her new haircut after all.

"I love it! Kay, this is great. Many of our Middle Eastern and East Asian clients don't drink. And don't even get me started on the recent college grads! They're, like, anti-liquor these days. But they love the drugs. Oh, they love drugs. But that's for a different day. Anyway, love, love, love!"

"Thanks, Liv! So, maybe you'll give me some advice. I've never done a promotional event." Olivia shared several ideas, like putting the drinks in ice buckets to make patrons feel VIP, creating neon Brunchies signs for photo ops, and giving free cans to anyone who posts to social media. Okay, they weren't the most innovative, but I appreciated her willingness to help.

After we ate, Olivia ran to the bathroom. I checked my phone again. Ever since Samantha couldn't get in touch with me that one time at Lola's, I became more cautious about my response time when I was out of the office. But nothing from Samantha. Just another message from Adam.

Adam: Hello…?

I experienced a rush of anxiety. I knew I shouldn't entertain him, but I wasn't sure I could get past my excitement either.

"What happened?" Olivia asked. "You look like you just saw a ghost." She sat down at the table.

"Oh, nothing. Just an old fling."

"Who? Adam? Are you still seeing him?"

"Wait, how'd you know I was ever seeing him?"

"He told Bryan you two were hanging out. But I thought that was a while ago." *What?* If Olivia knew, why hadn't she said anything?

"Um, yeah, you could say that." I tried to keep things vague.

"So you're seeing him again?"

"How'd you know we ever weren't?"

"Oh, I just assumed. Adam goes from girl to girl, so I figured you two would be a quick fling."

"Wait, why didn't you tell me that before?" I was genuinely shocked at her obliviousness, though maybe I shouldn't have been.

"What, did you catch feels for the guy?" Olivia asked accusatorily.

"No, no. Um, he just messaged me, and I hadn't heard from him in a while. That's all." I backtracked any hint of annoyance I showed. Knowing he and Bryan were friends, I was uncomfortable sharing more. That, and I'd hardly admitted to myself I was flirting with the idea of seeing Adam again. I didn't need Olivia to think I was.

"Ooooh, if you can lock him down..." Olivia said, her voice trailing like I'd be lucky to snatch him.

"What do you mean?"

"He's hot and rich." I hoped to get more insight from her, but she swiftly changed the subject. "Anyway, you still at Lola's?" I had a hunch she wanted to get information about Sisi because she hardly ever asked me questions about myself.

"Just a couple of times a week." Knowing Olivia wasn't a fan of Lola's, I downplayed how often I worked in some attempt to please her.

"No way! I don't know how you do it." She widened her eyes and sucked her teeth.

"Guess that means you don't ever think about coming back, huh?" I asked in an attempt to mitigate the tension.

"Oh, please, never. That place is a dump."

"Ha, yeah. Well, it helps pay the bills!" I scoffed, thinking I should have said, *Lucky you. You don't have to come back.* But for the second time today, I held my tongue. I was happy for her help on Brunchies and could at least appreciate that part of our lunch, if nothing else.

Dry

Working two jobs had been fine for some time, but with both of them ramping up, I really should've been slowing it down. Easier said than done, because I liked the extra cash and knew Sisi needed my help while hiring another manager. I planned to double down and trade in sleep for stress just a little while longer. *I'll be fine, right?*

The good news—Myra loved the Fourth of July party concept, along with the guest list I curated for it. The bad news—she wouldn't commit to LaToulle yet.

"Our team would like to see how this event goes before committing as a client. We love the idea of LaToulle, but candidly, we haven't seen a ton of investment from your team. Well, from Samantha," Myra said. I tried not to take her comment personal, though it felt that way. She was right. Samantha hadn't been responsive to emails. Since our initial call, it'd only been me corresponding with Myra and her associates, but I guess that wasn't enough.

"I totally understand. Samantha is not usually like this, but I promise I will make this party the best you've ever been to." And I meant it. Not the Samantha part, but that I'd put my all into this event.

"Glad to hear. Looking forward to seeing you there." I held on to Myra's bit of positivity, hoping I'd be able to redeem Samantha's indifference. I imagine Myra was shopping around for other PR reps. I just didn't know who she may be exploring. If I did, it'd prevent LaToulle from getting outshined.

—

When I arrived for an extra manager shift at Lola's on Thursday, I walked straight to Sisi's office. As usual, she was typing away on her laptop, only this time with a tall guy next to her. He wore a blue button-down tucked into a pair of dark jeans, and his dirty blond hair was recognizable as I got closer.

"Noah?"

"Kay! Twice this month. Lucky me." He turned around and leaned in for a hug.

"What are you doing here?" I asked.

"I'm an investor. Did you forget?" He had no problem reminding me he was in charge. "I heard you've been managing here. Leveling up, huh? What happened to your other gig?"

"It's not a gig. It's a PR firm. And I'm still there." I had a hard time discerning his ignorance for condescension.

"She's a mantender," Sisi joked before turning around to join us. "You know, a manager slash bartender." They both laughed, but I didn't find it particularly humoring.

"Noah is helping with my transition to head of operations, like showing me some of the financials, blah blah blah."

"Just happy to be here." Noah smiled.

"Anyway, Kay," Sisi continued. "I love when you work, but you've practically been living here! You must need some time off."

"That obvious, huh?" I guess I wasn't the only one who realized I'd been working a lot.

"I've never seen you look so exhausted. But maybe it's all that sex with Milo."

Embarrassing! I know I hadn't dated Noah in a while, but woah! Fortunately, he just grinned widely, knowing Sisi's comment was out of line. He looked adorable, and I remembered how he'd always used his light-hearted charm to slip out of the sticky situations he put himself in.

"Just do me a favor. Show Noah around real quick? It's been a while since he was here, and you know where all the restorations and repairs are," Sisi said.

"Yeah, sure. Let's go, Noah." I waved at him to follow me. I took him through the lounge and the kitchen and showed him the remodeled main floor. Over those fifteen minutes, we held the affable tension I recalled from when we went out together.

"All right, the last thing is the roof. Let's take the back stairs," I said.

"Oh, I remember the roof, all right." I assumed he was referring to one night last summer when the bar died down early. I was working alone when Noah came by. We had the roof to ourselves for a couple of hours and, after a few drinks, had sex overlooking the city. Slow, passionate, and hot.

I shook my head to rid myself of the memory and kept the tour moving. I walked up the narrow stairwell, my butt quickly meeting Noah's eyes as he followed me. In our silence, I heard the floorboards creak in a way I'd never noticed before. I felt more and more exposed with each step, knowing Noah was staring at my ass.

"So, that's it!" I said, gesturing my arm toward the roof, relieved when we reached the top. "I assume you don't have any questions."

"Well, actually, I do. But not about Lola's." He looked at me like, *You know what I mean.*

"Hm, what about?" I played dumb.

"Kay!" Sisi yelled from downstairs.

"Ah!" I shrieked, placing my hand over my heart. Noah laughed at how easily it startled me. Alarmed, we ran down the stairs.

"Are you done yet?" Sisi asked when we got back.

"Just finished!"

"That's it? That took no time."

"This isn't the Taj Mahal, Si. Anyway, what's up? You scared the shit out of me."

"Your munchies are here!" She pointed to the shipment I requested for the party.

"*Brunchies,* not *munchies.*" I rolled my eyes. "Wait! They're here?"

"Yeah, over there. I love their look!" Sisi gestured toward several large, hot pink boxes. They were the physical version of my design concept, inspired by our working session at Pink House. And they looked *so* good! I unboxed a case of the Miss Mosas, which came out even better than I hoped!

"Those are pretty fire," Noah chimed in. It warmed my heart to see their reactions. If Noah didn't believe my "gig" was important before, I'd at least hoped these redesigned cans showed him it was now.

"By the way, I don't need you all night. Wanna just stay for happy hour?" Sisi asked.

"Yeah, that's perfect!" Knowing Milo would be working a few more hours, I decided it was better to make extra cash while I waited for him.

"Cool. Though it's likely going to be slow."

"That's fine. I'm going to find fun ways to show off these cans at the party," I assured Sisi before she went upstairs to the kitchen.

"What party?" Noah asked after she left.

"I'm throwing a Fourth of July party for Brunchies," I said, holding up one of the Miss Mosas. "You're the investor. Shouldn't you know?"

"Hm, maybe you'll see me a third time this month." He lifted his eyebrows and smirked flirtatiously. I tried to repress my reciprocated smile and went upstairs for my bar shift, taking the package of Brunchies with me. *Oh, Noah, you always have a way of pulling me in.*

Before Milo arrived, he asked if I wanted takeout from a restaurant he'd been remodeling. Everywhere Milo went, people loved him. Especially his clients. He managed to bring us delicious meals and treats from them often.

> **Milo:** Here's the menu. Take your pick! But let me guess, the Greek salad with salmon.

> **Kay:** Mhmmmm. But you forgot the fries.

> **Milo:** Ah, the fries! Be there around eight.

Without a doubt, Milo was boyfriend material. I recognized it more and more over the past weeks. I became less afraid of what it meant to be with him because I knew he'd be a supportive and loving partner, but I was growingly uncertain about our connection. Would I get bored of his safety net?

"Hey, can you put in food for me?" Noah startled me. I'd forgotten he was here.

"Um, yeah, sure. What do you want?" Caught off guard, I wondered why of everyone working, he asked me.

"I actually don't remember the menu. Let me see." He came behind the bar, stood arm-to-arm with me, and looked at the computer screen.

"We have a paper menu." I inched away to pick one up for him.

"That's okay. I'd like to see the system anyway." Noah moved his fingers across the digital menu, and it was as if time had slowed down. Next to him, I felt a stream of affinity between us. He tilted his head toward me and hovered his hand above the entrée button.

"Here?" he asked, his eyes pierced through me. I felt a wave of fervor, remembering what it was like to be physically close to him.

"Yup." I remained casual, but there was no denying our connection. He turned his head back to the screen, his dirty blond hair tossing with it. Even without touching, I knew he wanted me. Our chemistry was electric. *Snap out of it, Kay.*

I peered across the main floor to see Milo waiting for me at the host stand. Seeing him, I was less than excited. In fact, I was bummed. Dramatic, but standing next to Noah again felt like nothing short of cosmic alignment. I didn't want to leave… *this.* Whatever *this* was.

"Is that the guy?" Noah asked.

"Oh, um. Well. That's Milo." As the words uncomfortably left my mouth, I knew I wished Noah didn't see him. Deep down, I wanted him to assume I was still single. *Why, when I finally have a nice guy, am I tested with temptation?*

After Milo and I shared dinner, we had mediocre sex. The initial magnetism I felt toward his body and his hips on mine was absent tonight. I further questioned if I needed something more. A little mystery, a little uncertainty, maybe?

I know, I know. We always ask for what we don't have, but sometimes a girl needs a little danger. And Milo is safe. *So safe.* I desired this kind of stability for so long, so why was I now so tempted to explore other options?

Milo and I lay together in silence that night. My mind shifted from responding to Adam, to the Brunchies party, to Noah, and ultimately, to maybe not committing to Milo after all. In the morning, he was gone. My first thought was one of relief. My second, *How is he?* I texted him on my way to work, enjoying the security of knowing that he'd always respond.

Garnished

———

For the first time in weeks, I put a lot of effort into my outfit for LaToulle's. I wore a flowy summer dress paired with a thin gold necklace and wedged sandals that forced me to take the bus.

Today was my first one-on-one video call with Samantha since she left for a sabbatical—I mean, "vacation." I dialed in for our 8:00 a.m. meeting early to accommodate her European time zone. With just a minute to spare, Andre swung open the door.

"She ain't makin' it." He looked at me blankly, like his words carried no significance.

"What?"

"She canceled all her meetings today. Let me guess, you didn't check your phone again this morning."

"Actually, I did!" I got defensive because I hadn't. I'd been listening to a podcast, trying to practice mindfulness on my commute.

"You really need a smartwatch or something," Andre huffed and went back to his desk. But true to his word, when I did check my phone, Samantha had messaged me.

> **Samantha:** Kay, need to postpone. I've asked Natasha to join you on the Brunchies event. She will be of help on-site. Let's debrief next week.

Her message was one of only a few I'd received from her all summer, but it irked me the most. She hadn't weighed in on any aspect of the event, yet somehow Natasha had to help?

Wait, Natasha has to help. At Lola's. Natasha at Lola's?

I shared my grievances with Sisi that evening before taking her to a Broadway show, a kind of "congratulations" for her promotion and a thank you for helping me climb out of debt and afford us a night out.

"I'm telling you, Samantha doesn't care about Brunchies. She sees how well you're doing and knows she doesn't have to worry. What you really need to be asking is whether a promotion is worth working for her."

"But what if—"

"But nothing! She's not going to change. It's been her firm for decades. Plus, how much more money do you think you'll make there? I haven't heard of her treating anyone how they're valued. Hasn't Andre been in the same role for, like, twenty years?" I wanted to convince her Samantha wasn't so bad, but my phone buzzed.

> **Olivia:** We're having a party on Saturday at Tap. Come!

I showed Sisi and told her about Olivia's new haircut and business relationship with Bryan, and that she even helped me with ideas for the Brunchies party. Sisi wasn't impressed.

"Oh please, it'll always only be about Olivia. Olivia, Olivia, Olivia. Period. But I do want to see her hair, so show me!" I pulled up Olivia's recent TikTok. "She does look good, I'll give her that." She took my phone to scroll through the comments when I got another message. "Seriously, you're talking to that dude?"

Adam: Where's Kay?

"Not even! I haven't heard from him for days."
"So you're not messaging him?"
"Well, no."
"Why so sus?"
"No, I haven't, I swear! But honestly… I've thought about it. Look, before you give me crap, I get that Milo is great. I know that, you know that, I think the whole world knows that. But Si, it's easy and safe and, well…"
"Boring?" she asked.
"A little…" I sighed, knowing how unfortunate the circumstance was. "I finally have a great guy who I really love spending time with, but I'm just not sure…"
"Then just see Adam." *Seriously?*
"Seriously?" I asked again, this time out loud.
"You've been so unsure about Milo—which is crazy, by the way—so why not go and get this loser out of your system? Maybe if you're with Adam again, you'll finally realize how good you have it and move on." I didn't have a chance to respond because we arrived at the theater and the usher hurried us to our seats.

"The show is starting!" She whispered angrily. When we sat, I texted Adam back.

Kay: What's up?

I wasn't sure what it would lead to, but Milo was out of town this weekend for a beach trip. I figured now was a better time than ever.

During intermission, I got confirmation from Milo that he'd arrived at the beach, though I was more excited to see a flurry of messages from Adam.

Adam: Finally. Thought you were dodging me.

Adam: I want to see you again.

Adam: When are you free?

Adam: Can I see you?

Kay: Maybe.

As tempted as it'd been, I didn't think I could carry through. Sure, Milo and I weren't "official" yet, but it didn't dismiss Adam's intolerable actions just a few months prior.

Throughout the second act, I tried to remember this, though truthfully, I couldn't resist thinking about what would happen if I turned my *maybe* into a *yes*. Either way, Adam didn't need to know that yet.

Bottom's Up

The next morning, I lay spread out across my mattress and stared out my bedroom window. I found pleasure in having my apartment to myself again, without Milo. It didn't seem normal to feel contained at the start of a budding relationship. I tried to shake the feeling.

On the other hand, today was the perfect day for the Brunchies event. The sun beamed, and the temperature was warm but not too hot. I made a strong coffee, worked out, and dressed in my best outfit for the long evening ahead. After the Brunchies event, I promised Olivia I'd go to her and Bryan's party at Tap, a chic club downtown.

I wore a strapless blue and white top that tied like a bow at my chest with dark blue, shimmery shorts. I omitted red so as not to appear too matchy, and I made sure my outfit wasn't too revealing. Myra would be at Lola's, and I wanted her to know I was more professional than our situation rendered.

Sisi insisted I come as a guest, not an employee. In return, I'd make sure all the drinks were placed where they needed to be. Kind of my job anyway as the PR rep, but also my best option so Natasha wouldn't uncover my second job. I predetermined the best thing to do would be to play it cool.

It was unlikely Natasha would find out anyway, between her withdrawn attitude and that she'd only be managing the guest list.

The party started at 3:00 p.m. and would end after the 9:00 p.m. annual fireworks, which we'd watch from the rooftop. When I arrived, Sisi, in a blue and sparkly latex romper and white boots, directed an electrician to install red, white, and blue light fixtures across the rooftop.

"Yes, like that! That's perfect!" she told him before showing the hired burlesque artists where they'd perform in a few hours.

I got to work immediately, strategically placing the Brunchies cans inside matching buckets with decorates aligned to the flavor, like sprinkling peach candies with the Peach-a-lini. The entire staff also worked together, listening to pop music, rolling silverware, and preparing the cash registers. It was the excitement before an ensuing night that was often the best part.

"Are these seriously the new drinks you want us to serve? There's no alcohol in them." One of the waitresses said to Sisi and I, just as I was greeting Natasha. *Perfect timing.*

"What's wrong with it?" Sisi asked.

"Just weird." She shrugged and walked away. *Ugh.* Her comment ruminated with me, and I felt like I'd been sucker punched. Sisi rolled her eyes and turned back to me.

"These bitches and their opinions," she said before storming off to address another matter. I only hoped Brunchies would be better received by our guests, especially in front of Myra.

And to no avail, they were. About an hour into the party, the rooftop was full but not overcrowded. Natasha fulfilled her role of managing the guest list effectively. Each lounge area had a group of five to ten friends who purchased a table in advance.

It was a calmer environment than the jungle themed party, and everyone seemed to take to Brunchies. I even heard a few people give compliments like, "How cute are these?" and "Perfect! I didn't want to get wasted today." As I was saving their quotes on my Notes app, Myra arrived.

"This is very impressive," she said, looking around.

"Myra, it's so nice to see you again!" And it was because she was happy, which made me relieved. Regardless of Samantha's nonattendance, there was no denying my event was a success.

"I think this is great. I know you said this isn't only about photos, but I'm going to snap a few."

"Oh, please, go ahead! I also put a Polaroid on each table instead of hiring a photographer. Thought it would better capture the mood we want to strike."

"Ah, agreed. Love it!" she said.

—

Another hour later, the doors closed, Natasha left, and the burlesque performance began. A man juggling knives and eating fire started the routine, followed by a drag performance and ending with two women dancing in panties and pasties. I looked around at the fun-loving crowd until my eyes met with Noah's. I felt a jolt in my heart. *He actually came?*

I pretended I didn't see him and checked in with Myra, who stood with me at the end of the show. As we watched together, she clapped with the crowd, which made the nearly visible boobs swinging in front of us a lot less awkward. And just as the performers reached the peak of their act, someone tapped my shoulder. I jumped, worried it was Noah.

"Ah! Girl, it's been a damn minute." It was Lilly, the writer at *Moxy*, her English accent more pronounced than ever. "How are you?" she asked before hugging me. "And Myra, hello! Brunchies is fabulous!" she said before air kissing her.

"Lilly, what are you doing here?" I asked, knowing she was supposed to be in the Hamptons this weekend.

"Ah, we decided not to go. The traffic was out of control, and we'd never make it to our party in time." She said "we," speaking to the woman next to her, whom I didn't recognize.

"Hi, I'm Tiffany," the woman introduced herself. She was a middle-aged Black woman, elegant in her expensive jewelry and designer dress, assured in her warm greeting and a firm handshake.

"Tiffany is the head of commercial marketing for Moxy Media," Lilly told us. "And I am just lucky enough to be doing a feature on her and her fabulousness."

"Oh, please," Tiffany rebutted humbly. "Great event here. I like it," she continued. We introduced ourselves and our line of work, which Tiffany was very interested in. She especially wanted to learn more about the event.

"So, who's throwing this party? It's really just fabulous, and I love the way you're debuting Brunchies," she said.

"LaTou—" I started to answer when Myra interrupted.

"It was all Kay. She put this together," she leaned in, covering the side of her mouth to sarcastically whisper, "even though her boss is terrible." I nervously laughed, her comment more uncomfortable than the swinging burlesque boobs.

"Unsupportive bosses get you nowhere. Lilly, send Kay my email," she ordered. "I'd like to tell you about a role we have on my team. I think there's a place for this kind of talent at *Moxy*." I was in disbelief. Her offer came so quickly, but Tiffany had that type of captivating presence. I imagine she was someone who rarely heard the word "no." So, I nodded, even though it felt like I was cheating on Samantha.

"If she lived in Austin, I'd offer her a role too!" Myra added. "Was nice meeting you ladies, but I've got another party to head to. Kay, I'll be in touch with you and Samantha by Tuesday. Let me talk to my team first, but I can't iterate enough: You nailed it." She patted me on the shoulder and waved goodbye to us all.

"Come, let's have a drink!" Lilly suggested. She pulled me to the bar, where there were a few Brunchies sitting atop it.

"So, you like the new branding?" I asked her, showing off the Hail Mary can.

"They seriously look *so* great! So much better than in Austin. I actually want to drink it now!" We both laughed

"Well, thank you." I bowed my head to insinuate it was my idea.

"You did this? Look at you, girl!"

"After our night in Austin, I pitched Myra, and this party is my attempt to show them LaToulle should be their PR firm. But my boss never showed," I admitted.

"No way! All the more reason to take Tiffany up on her offer. She is just a delight to work for. You need someone like her to be your champion, your mentor. I'll make sure there's a meeting arranged for you two." I smiled, envisioning what it'd be like to leave LaToulle. I'd held on to the prospect of a promotion for so long that the thought of leaving hadn't crossed my mind before.

Lilly and I opted for a real cocktail next, which quickly became two, and the next thing I knew, the rooftop was cheering, "*Sisi! Sisi!*" We checked the crowd only to find Sisi in the middle of it, shimmying with the burlesque dancers. I laughed out loud with Lilly, then Sisi spotted me. She motioned her finger as if I should join her, which would not be happening, no matter how many drinks I'd had. I slipped toward the back of everyone to hide.

I steeped my shoulders into my ears, sipped my drink, and looked out over the rooftop. With the red, white, and blue lights illuminating the sky and everyone wearing skimpier outfits in the summer haze, Lola's had transformed into an erotic venue, as if its reputation as an elite lounge normalized the seduction induced atmosphere in the air tonight. Just in time, the fireworks started. I turned with the crowd to watch when I felt someone next to me.

"I like your outfit." It was Noah, looking at me with a smile in his eyes but not on his mouth. I felt unshielded, like when he trailed behind me on the stairs the other day. Only this time, in Lola's erotic haze, I was more tempted than ever before. The thought of being intimate with him again flushed my mind.

"Kay! You should have joined me out there!" Sisi said, interrupting mine and Noah's gaze. She glistened with sweat, her hair messy, and her fake eyelash shifted off her eyelid. I looked at her like, *Yeah, right.*

"So, you're keeping the party going then?" I asked her.

"No way! It's gone on long enough. The fireworks are over, and I want these people out soon."

"What? After all that shimmying?"

"Definitely. I've revealed enough tonight. So, they don't have to go home, but by eleven, they've got to get the hell out of here!" The timing worked out perfectly because I needed to meet Olivia downtown. I tried Sisi one more time.

"Sure you don't want to come with me to Liv's party?"

"Hmm…" Sisi pretended to contemplate my question. "Nah!"

"Where are you going?" Noah asked.

"You two keep chatting. I think the burlesque performers want their cash." When Sisi stepped away, I told Noah about Olivia's party.

"Do you want to go?" The moment I asked, I wondered if I'd regret it.

"Yeah, I'll come."

And for the second time tonight, I felt like I was cheating.

Shaken… and Stirred

———

There is something euphoric about knowing you have a man's attention as if you're the only woman to exist in his orbit. That's how I felt with Noah in the cab on our way to Tap. Being tipsy only amplified it.

On opposite sides of the backseat, Noah placed his hand on my left thigh and squeezed it gently. I couldn't resist putting my hand on top of his. We rested our heads back and tilted them toward each other. He had a look of insatiable desire in his eyes.

We'd been together many times before, but this time felt different. Like we both wanted to share everything about ourselves—our romances, needs, and what we desired in bed—in a way we never had before. But we couldn't. We arrived at Tap too soon.

"All right, you two, this is it," the driver muffled in a raspy voice. Noah led me out of the car first and placed his hand on my lower back. I basked in the moment, knowing, for right now, I was his.

Tap had a speakeasy vibe, with its entranceway masked by a decadent flower shop storefront filled with roses, hydrangeas, and snake plants. Olivia added me to the VIP list, which waived my entry fee, though the real treat was bypassing the line of people wrapped around the building. A hostess guarding the private door so many waited to enter let us in right away.

Inside the lounge, antique wallpaper wrapped the walls in varying shades of a sepia tone. The couches were a deep plum color. Above them, rose gold mirrors. The music was electric—a variation of Brazilian jazz and house music. But there was also another glaring feature at tonight's event. Searching for Olivia and Bryan, I saw Brunchies on every table, beautifully placed in all-white ice buckets.

"Kay, here!" Olivia spotted me in the crowd. She led Noah and me to her table, where she handed us the newly rebranded Brunchies cans.

"How did you get these here?" I asked, totally perplexed.

"Oh, Bryan did! I told him they hadn't signed with LaToulle, so he pitched Myra as a potential client, but at a much lower fee. Actually, you just missed her! She stopped by for a little bit but left." I stood silent, dumbfounded in disbelief by her nonchalant, almost braggy, response. "I know, right? You think she'd stay longer, but apparently, this 'wasn't her scene,'" Olivia said, airing quotation marks with her index and middle fingers. "I mean, come on. Look how good it all looks. I know we don't have *all* the bells and whistles like LaToulle, but we tried! We even hired a photographer! Anyway, come, I want you to meet everyone!"

Before I could ask any questions, she brought Noah and me to her table, poured us both a huge shot, and introduced her new friends and cast members from her upcoming show. I didn't know how to feel about any of it. On one hand, Brunchies wasn't my client yet. On the other, Olivia swooped them up from under me without so much as a mention.

I headed to the bathroom to collect my thoughts, but as I made my way through the crowd, I felt a tight grip on my arm. It was Noah, visibly more intoxicated but handsome as ever.

"Where are you going?" He pulled me toward him to dance. There we were, in the crowd, away from everyone else, embracing our inner desire. He spun me around to face him and pulled me close to his body. His smirk faded, and his demeanor changed. I didn't have a moment to resist. And, truly, I didn't want to. The music slowed, and so did we. He pressed his body against mine, and I weakened. I wanted more.

"I'm glad you came," I said.

"I wanted to spend more time with you," he responded. The music rose, and strobe lights lit up the otherwise pitch-black room. I faced the other way, my back on Noah. The beat dropped, and the crowd began jumping. The lights beamed all over. In one moment, I could see the room; the next, I was blinded.

Noah grabbed my waist and spun me toward him again. We went still as the crowd moved around us. He grabbed my chin and lightly raised my head. I looked into his eyes as the lights flickered on and off his face. I had never had more lust for someone before. I completely forgot about Brunchies.

He continued to stare, and it felt as if time had stopped. His eyes pierced through me, and a jolt of ecstasy ran through my body. He leaned in further, his kiss deep, passionate, and lasting for what felt like a minute. The room spun around us as his hands gripped my back tighter. I could feel him on me. It made me quiver. Excited for everything that could be, forgetting about what was. I wanted so much more, but he stopped me.

"I shouldn't do this," he said.

What?

"I'm seeing someone, and I think it could be serious. Sorry, Kay." He walked off the dance floor and left me alone, shocked, among the strangers around me. Unsure of what to do, I walked back to Olivia's table. I joined them for another shot and shook it off. Noah had always been unattainable. What made tonight any different?

"Where were you? Come dance!" Olivia said.

"Um, just one second." I grabbed my phone to decompress for a moment. I had a missed call from Milo. *Of course.* I held my index finger and pinky to my ear and motioned my lips to Olivia, *Need to make a call.* But before I could, Bryan joined the table.

"I was wondering when you'd get here. Was that your boyfriend out there?" *Shit. I guess someone did see me.* My face must have conveyed my anxiety because Bryan changed the subject. "Oh, sorry, I didn't know. I just assumed... Um, hey, thanks for passing on Brunchies, they're a killer team, and I got a nice commission out of it." Bryan was clearly oblivious to Olivia's antics, but I wasn't. She used Brunchies, at my expense, to get closer to him.

"Kay makes pennies at LaToulle! You should get her a job!" Olivia interrupted. "She even needs to bartend on the side. It's so awful." *What the fuck, Olivia.*

"That's so cool. You work in the industry too! I didn't know you could do that. I'd bartend if I could. Bet you make great money." At least Bryan had a decent enough response to all of this, but it didn't excuse the situation I found us both in.

"Ha, yeah."

Without another word, I went to the bathroom, this time to pee. Then, I planned to leave. *Why didn't I listen to Sisi?*

While I waited in line, I peeked at the DJ stand only to notice a familiar face. Adam. He saw me, too, and he wasted no time coming over.

"Hey, stranger," he said, his masculine voice penetrating, his words landing softly amid the high-energy crowd. "Didn't think I'd see you here."

"Oh, hey. Olivia told me to come." I reciprocated with kindness, remembering I hadn't responded to his last message. Then, my phone rang again. It was Milo

"Is that the new guy?" Adam asked, looking at my phone light up in my hand.

"Yeah, maybe." I smiled uncomfortably. Adam looked at me like, *I hope you don't answer,* before he put his arm around my shoulders. I smelled his body wash, the same one I used when I stayed at his apartment. In an instance, I was taken back to our spontaneous date nights.

"I missed you," he said. I wasn't sure if it was the alcohol, the yearning for physical touch outside of Milo's, or my lack of self-restraint for Adam, but I let him take me behind the DJ booth. I stayed there the rest of the night and didn't return Milo's call. I was doing to him what so many guys had done to me but lacked the sympathy to fester on it anymore tonight. I shot him a simple text instead.

> **Kay:** Busy night at Lola's! Talk tomorrow, have fun <3.

With my better sense out the window, I joined Adam at his apartment after Tap. Being there felt foreign yet familiar. We sat on his dark couch with the lights dim, and the aroma from his wax candle consumed the air. Adam crept his hand over my blue shorts, under my shirt, and up my belly. He leaned in and kissed me as he put his other arm around my back. My body shivered. I was instantly wet.

I laid my body back, and Adam extended his other arm to turn on the record player. Smooth R & B played around us as his tongue met mine. Slowly, his body climbed on top of me. I wrapped my arms around his shoulders and moved them down his upper back. His waist moved above mine. His hardness rubbed over my thigh and then onto my center. Adam slowly gelled into me, and I swore my wetness seeped through my shorts, which he quickly pulled down as I took off his shirt.

In a swift motion, Adam lifted me from the couch to his bed a few feet over. My legs wrapped around his waist, and my arms gripped his bare back while he pulled us down. I loved to feel his back and neck as he nestled in my chest. I undid his pants and pulled them down slightly to his thighs before pushing them off completely with my foot. His briefs were the only thing between us. I couldn't bear the wait any longer, so I took them off and pushed myself toward his bareness. He was so hard. It made me want him right away.

But he made me wait. He got up to pull out a mirror from behind his wardrobe, which he propped up next to the bed, positioning it in front of us. Undressed, I couldn't help but think, *Has he done this before?*

Without time to dwell, his hardness was back on top of me. Only this time, I could see everything I was feeling. We watched ourselves until I climaxed, and he quickly after.

"You're so hot," he muttered. I ran to the bathroom to avoid a UTI. When I came back to his king bed, I saw him asleep. I rolled my eyes and lay down next to him. I checked my phone to see I had three more messages.

Milo: Just let me know you got home okay.

Milo: Kay?

Milo: Okay, I'm home. Guess we'll just talk tomorrow.

I wondered how I managed to have a romantic night by textbook standards, only to feel isolated, alone, and used—all as I lay next to someone else. I slid my phone on the nightstand and dozed off.

—

The sunlight woke me the next morning, almost hitting me harder than the guilt. Hungover and tired, I rolled over to see Adam sprawled across the bed. With him, I felt so alone, palpable as I stumbled across the apartment to the bathroom. Men's face wash. Anything to cleanse myself.

When I came out, Adam was up and watering his plants as if nothing were out of the ordinary. Like I stayed with him often, and this was routine.

"You're up." His deep voice was less appealing today.

"I'm up." I found my clothes layered next to the bed. I'd have to wear last night's holiday attire this early morning. "Do you water them every morning?" I asked, hoping to soften the tension that potentially only I felt.

"Plants do need water." He lifted his eyebrows and continued tilting the water can toward them. I knew they meant more to him than I did.

"Where are you going?" He asked when I walked to his front door.

"I have a lot to do today." I turned the doorknob to leave.

"Hey, wait a sec," he said. I turned back and gave him a moment to initiate something. But nothing. I got nothing.

Months later, and I still couldn't get a read on Adam. I attempted to open the door again. He stopped me again, this time extending his hand down my right arm and around my waist, toward him, signaling not to leave.

"As much as I would have loved this before, I really need to go, Adam. This isn't what I want." I was proud of my directness, regardless of how it came out.

After I left, Adam watched me walk down the hall, like the way he watched me the first time we met. Only this time, I wanted no part in it. In a mere few hours, any lust I had for Adam was gone. In fact, I couldn't wait for Milo to come home.

Hangover

New York City is always a ghost town during the Fourth of July weekend, but this year its silence fell on me. I was left to obsess over my upcoming meeting with Samantha, Olivia's aloofness, and my conflicted feelings about Milo.

On Tuesday, when Milo returned from his trip and still hadn't made plans with me, I asked him to spend the night. He told me it'd been a long, long weekend, and he needed rest. I assumed he felt some type of way about my screening his call and subsequent messages on Saturday. Otherwise, I imagine he would be more excited to see me. Suppose I only had myself to blame for that.

At LaToulle, I refocused my attention, because today I had my meeting with Samantha. I was eager to tell her about the Brunchies party, otherwise known as "the calm before my weekend storm." Then, as it became routine, Andre interjected beforehand.

"I saw you had a fun weekend." *What could he possibly be talking about?* "You know, at the party."

"Which party?" I tried not to be defensive, but Andre loved knowing more than others around him, and this felt invasive.

"The Brunchies party. I saw the photos. You looked great." *Shoot. The photographer. But which event, and who sent Samantha photos?*

"Can you send me what you saw?" I asked him.

"Oh, sweetie. I can't do that. They're Samantha's private emails."

"Seriously?" My tone dropped along with my head.

"Well, I *can* walk away and let you use my desktop." I hated that he dangled this over me. It was almost time for my rescheduled meeting with Samantha, but this was essential, so I gave in. Andre opened the file before "grabbing a tea," so I was left with his computer. In the attachment, there were seven hundred-plus photos from Tap. I could have died.

One by one, I scrolled through. Photo one hundred fifty-one, I appeared for the first time. There I was, walking in with Noah. *Okay, not bad.* And there was another photo, one hundred eighty-four through one hundred eighty-six. Olivia and I were getting ready to take a photo, taking a photo, then talking to one another postphoto. *Okay, still not bad.*

I continued scrolling into the mid-three hundreds. "Wait, Kay, go back," Andre said, peering over my shoulder unexpectedly. I guess his tea run was over. I scrolled back slowly through a few photos. "Right there," he said.

"What?" All I saw were people smiling in front of the dance floor.

"Oooh, he is cute, girl." Andre pointed to the very corner of the photo. I wasn't sure how he spotted me, but there I was, kissing Noah.

"Oh my god! Oh. My. God," I let out. What at the time was sexy was now super cringy.

"Would you calm down? No one will see that. There's, like, a million photos," Andre said, finally showing some compassion.

After scrolling through another hundred photos, I only had five minutes until my meeting. Over those minutes, Andre and I paced through the rest of the images. There were a few of me dancing in the distance, but they were hardly recognizable. And, of course, there was Adam. He and I were standing side-by-side with one another, one shot indicating there was a romantic intrigue, at least to me.

"When did Samantha get these? Do you think she saw them?" I began spiraling.

"You need to get on your time zones, girlie. Myra's back in Austin and sent that late last night to Samantha and cc'd you. I'm just trying to teach you a lesson. You need to check your emails in the morning!"

"Okay, seriously? Now is not the time for a lecture! What did her message say?" I asked. Andre widened his eyes and changed his demeanor back to compassion.

"Don't worry, it's good! It's a good email! Your meeting with Samantha is now... Just read it after. Here, I got conference room C for you." I wanted to scream. How in a city so big could something like this unfold in one night?

Waiting for Samantha to join the Zoom, I continued to panic. I felt my breakfast move in my stomach and my hands sweat. *Did she know more? Would she care? Was I fired?* I looked out the floor-to-ceiling windows, the sky cloudy and drizzling. It all didn't feel so glamorous.

"Kay! It's been some time." Samantha joined suddenly, which jolted me from my seat.

"Oh, hi, Samantha!" My heart could have pumped out of my chest. I turned from the window to the monitor, where her face projected.

"So, tell me. Sounds like the event went well." She was the bubbliest I'd seen her. If her engagement rumor were true, it sure did look good on her.

"It went really well! Myra loved the whole thing, and I think we did all we could to show her we understand her vision and can make it happen." I said, feeding off Samantha's high energy. I assumed because she didn't mention the photos immediately, she hadn't seen them after all.

"Perfect. Did you see her email yet?"

"Um, no, not yet."

"Well, seems she loved the event too. She just wasn't so pleased about my missing it. But, oh well! Nothing we can do about that now, can we?" This was a potential client opportunity, so it surprised me how easily she brushed it off. I wondered if her nebulousness jeopardized my effort to land the Brunchies account. "Actually, Kay, you might want to read it, because guess what?" *No, please don't say the photos.* "We landed the account. Myra wants LaToulle to represent Brunchies." My roller coaster of emotions just hit its peak.

"Wait, really?" I asked, truly shocked. I knew the event was a success, but I wasn't expecting Myra to make her decision so soon. I mean, the party at Tap was also impressive.

"Why are you so surprised?"

"I'm just happy is all!" I tamed my reaction. I didn't want Samantha to ever find out I went to the competing party or was making out at it.

"Oh yes, read the email. She loved that our event was fun but tasteful. Apparently, the other rep she considered was immature, fighting with his girlfriend or something. Oh, and it was late at night. She doesn't think the brand is meant for late-night parties. It's a day to evening kind of drink. But she did like the venue! You'll see. She sent photos." *Shit.* "But I won't have time to go through them. Doesn't matter. Just find out where they were and add it to our pitch list. Oh, and never higher a photographer. She hated that about the other event but loved your Polaroid idea. Nice touch!" *Phew.* She didn't see the photos, and I don't think she ever would. "All said, good work. I knew I could rely on you while I've been away."

"Thank you!" I didn't want to divulge any more than I needed to, and Samantha's aloofness toward my work allowed me not to.

"Anyway, I'll get back to Myra, letting her know you'll be her main point of contact. Let's get moving on local press and send her ideas for some mocktail experiences that are TikTok friendly."

"Yes, of course. On it," I knew this would be a huge undertaking and wondered if it meant I landed the promotion. But I didn't ask. At least not yet. I needed more composure and self-assurance. So, Samantha and I discussed contract formalities, and I updated her on some of our work with Henry's. And just when I thought my emotional roller coaster ride was over, Samantha asked me something I wasn't expecting.

"Now, let me talk to you about something else," she said. "Is there a reason you didn't tell me you have two jobs?" My stomach sank into my butt. Again. I'd become so comfortable with working at Lola's, I'd forgotten that no one I worked with knew about my second income.

Before I could answer, she continued, "Do we not pay you enough here?" I wanted to say, *Of course you don't! How does anyone get by in New York City on a $65,000 salary?* Instead, I put my head down, embarrassed. "Or, if it's the benefits, let me know. You are a star, Kay! And we want you here."

Samantha came across nervous and a bit desperate, a side of her I hadn't seen before. I felt bad that she felt bad, even though her comment was willfully ignorant. Then, I had a thought. *Despite Samantha's confidence with her wardrobe, clients, and lifestyle, was she insecure about others perceiving her as a bad boss?*

I knew what I wanted to say, but I sat there in silence. She'd made the fact I worked at Lola's only about her. Still, she pressed me again, "Kay? Do you have anything to say?"

"Oh, yes, yes!" I responded overenthusiastically.

"Yes, what?" she asked.

"Yes, I should have told you I had another job. I just didn't want you to think I couldn't handle it." I smelled the phoniness on my breath because I also wanted to say, *Clients love me! I'm available by email. If only you knew how well I'd done despite working over seventy hours a week!* But I didn't say any of that. I was too nervous and, frankly, just happy she didn't see the photos of me sucking face with Noah.

"I won't ask you to divulge your circumstance, but we are here for you." Samantha extended her hand toward the camera as if to offer me a virtual gesture of sincerity.

I assumed she thought of me as a sad, young girl desperate for cash. I felt ashamed to be viewed in such a compromising light and wasn't sure if she wanted me to quit Lola's or not. Without anything more to contribute, we ended our call without a solution. A few hours later, a company-wide email went out.

If any employee has a second job, volunteer position, or joins a political campaign, please inform management as part of our new policy.

They probably added the volunteer or campaign disclosure in an effort not to isolate me, but it didn't work. I still felt awful and knew the office gossip would swirl. If no one knew about Lola's before, I'm sure they would now.

As a mental break from my self-sabotaging thoughts, I had another one—*how did Samantha know about Lola's?*

Straight Up

After work—without a shift at Lola's or plans with Milo—I needed to go somewhere far from the city to escape my thoughts. So, I took a bus to New Jersey. Okay, a twenty-minute commute across the Hudson River isn't so far, but it was the distance I needed to get perspective on the chaos I experienced in Manhattan.

As the bus drove from New York Port Authority to Jersey City, I watched the sun set over the Manhattan skyline. It reflected a beautiful orange hue across the array of skyscrapers. I planned to walk the boardwalk along the river, but on my way, I stumbled upon a grandiose doorway in the middle of the street. What at first looked like a church, the tall wooden door was accompanied by a gold Buddha statue next to it. A small street sign blown over a few feet away read, "Meditation Center." *Was this a literal sign?*

Inside, a girl with dark hair and clean makeup greeted me. Her voice was calm and welcoming. "Hi! Are you here for a drop-in class?"

"Um, yes." Given I'd "dropped in," I thought, *Why not?* I paid ten dollars and entered a second, beaded doorway that led to a wide, circular room with a goldplated dome ceiling.

In the center were stairs that led to two open floors below, with about fifty people spread throughout them. It amazed me that a place like this existed. Usually I'd walk by, and it'd go unnoticed, but my curiosity in a different city allowed me to uncover it.

An echoing gong let out from downstairs, and people began to follow it. I assumed the sound signaled class was starting. I joined everyone on the bottom floor and followed a narrow corridor to another expansive room. In it, everyone sat cross-legged over a pillow on the floor.

"Here, take this." A man who looked like he was in his mid-forties handed me a faded pink pillow. "And don't forget to take off your shoes," he whispered.

"Thank you," I whispered back and took my seat. A woman at the front of the room hit the gong again. Then again, and again, lighter each time. Everyone bowed their heads, and I followed suit. A person wearing a blue cloak held a thick Victorian-era type book and walked from the doorway to the center of the room, where a pillow was propped in front of several Buddhas.

"Ohm," the class chanted in unison. I joined them a bit too late and held my ohm a bit too long. *They should have a guide for beginners.*

The instructor read a few quotes about mindfulness. Then, silence. It gripped the room. I wasn't sure how long the class would last, so after a few minutes of uncertainty, I embraced it. I closed my eyes and allowed my thoughts to battle for space in my mind until they ultimately cleared. Lost in a trance, the gong startled me when it went off again. I opened my eyes to see the instructor was gone.

Slowly, people rose and exited to a common area where mint tea was served. *All this for $10? Hello, Jersey!* I checked the clock and saw three hours had passed. It was already 9:30 p.m.!

"Surprised at the time?" the man who offered me a cushion asked. "It must be your first time here."

"How could you tell?" I asked sarcastically. He laughed.

"What'd you come here for?"

"I actually stumbled on this place, but it came at a good time."

"Oh, and why is that?" he asked, pouring us both tea.

"Well, I'm a certified people pleaser," I said, sarcastic again.

"People pleasers don't think they're good enough." He was matter of fact.

"You don't say?" I raised my eyebrows and took the teacup from him.

"Almost cost me my marriage years ago. For the longest time, I didn't think I was worthy of my wife. I thought of other possibilities, other women. But it was me all along. I had to learn I was worthy of someone loving me." He sipped his tea. I'd usually find the open discussion with a stranger odd, but the meditation center created a relaxed space where this type of conversation almost felt encouraged.

Another gong went off. "Are you going to the second part of the class?" he asked.

"Another session? It's almost ten at night!"

"We do an extra hour on Tuesdays to seal the practice."

"I think I'm sealed. But it was nice to meet you." I didn't catch his name, but his words ruminated with me when I left the class.

I walked to the Hudson River and looked over the big city skyline. I realized how small my world was within it. I thought about how many people lived in the two-mile metropolis and all the different lives we led. Here, you could be anyone you wanted—so why wasn't I doing that? I had always wanted others' approval, worrying what they thought or waiting for them to make me happy. Not anymore. From now on, I'd prioritize myself first, starting by splurging on a yellow cab home.

Hair of the Dog

My evening in Jersey City fueled me with a fresh perspective. I wouldn't let anyone else determine my fate so easily anymore, starting with confronting those who were. Step one—Natasha. On top of being a difficult colleague, I was convinced she found out about Lola's during the Brunchies event and told Samantha.

"Natasha. I need to talk to you." I faced her desk, adjacent to mine.

"Yeah, okay, grab time on my calendar." She looked at her computer screen, ignoring my presence.

"No, let's talk now. It's important." Without a clap back, we walked to the same conference room I'd had my call with Samantha yesterday. Today, the sun shined, and the city was more vibrant underneath us as Manhattanites were back from their holiday weekends.

"I'm just going to come out with it. You've been difficult to work with. I've tried and tried, but… What's going on?" I expected her to be combative or defensive, but Natasha let out a sigh, almost like she was relieved.

"Well, I—" She stopped and swallowed a lump in her throat. "Let me think about how to say this…" She paused. I waited, unfazed by her silence.

"Okay, since you started, I've been in your shadow. On your first day, Samantha told me to follow you. I've just felt like I've had something to prove ever since you joined."

"That makes two of us, but it doesn't mean I put you down or keep you iced out of emails."

"Okay, you're right, but it doesn't mean you've been much better." A defensiveness arose from her depths. *Here we go.*

"What do you mean, I haven't been much better?"

"Kay, you don't look at me as your counterpart. You may copy me on emails, but you never ask me for my advice or ideas. I have a work history before this, too, and I know a lot more than you might think. Before I came here, I worked at a resort in Montreal."

"You were a bartender too?" I asked.

"What do you mean? I was a wedding planner." *Of course she was.* "Wait, you were a bartender?" she asked.

"Oh please, like you don't already know." She looked puzzled, like she truly had no idea I worked at Lola's. "Wait, you don't know?"

"I have no idea what you're talking about." I could tell she wasn't lying, so I told her about my history at Lola's, then about my conversation with Samantha yesterday.

"That's actually pretty admirable. I don't think I'd have it in me for a second job. But how cool! Bartending seems like a lot of fun."

"Ha, yeah. It can be." *If she wasn't the one who said anything, who did?*

"Pff, even with two jobs, you're still going to get a promotion." Natasha widened her eyes.

"What do you mean?"

"Kay, it's obvious you're getting the client lead role." I almost felt guilty that Natasha knew I was a better employee than her, but the feeling quickly faded when I realized how hard I'd worked for it, though I was no longer convinced it mattered. Did I really want to work for a woman who pitied my work ethic?

"I'm only in this role because my aunt is friends with Samantha," Natasha admitted. "She'll probably never promote me. She thinks I'm just lucky to be here, kind of like Andre. The only difference is I don't bow down to this place like he does."

"What do you mean?"

"When I asked Samantha if I was being considered for client lead, she flat out said, 'Not this year, but keep sticking around. LaToulle is a fabulous job for your résumé.'"

"Well, it doesn't seem like you love it here anyway. Why do you keep pushing it?" I asked bluntly—no more sugarcoating.

"I think I want to prove myself." She paused. "You know, you remind me a lot of my sister, Bri. This is super cringy to say, but I've always been jealous of her, and I think I put that on you. You didn't deserve that. Well, you don't deserve that." Natasha shifted her head down in what was officially the most vulnerable I'd seen her.

"That couldn't have been easy to admit. So, thank you. It means a lot." Natasha continued to look down. "Let's call it water under the bridge. From now on, you copy me on emails, and I'll ask your advice." I attempted to lighten the mood, which was effective, because Natasha laughed.

"And I'll stop being a jealous bitch," she shot back jokingly.

Later, we went to lunch and had a fun time laughing about clients and talking about her new girlfriend. I just hoped our friendship would continue, whether I stayed at LaToulle or not.

Step two—I texted Olivia. I could've listened to Sisi a long time ago and cut her out to avoid all this, but it was too late for that now. To keep up with my commitment not to ghost people, I'd break off our friendship the right way—in person.

Over coffee that afternoon, our conversation started out light. However, things quickly turned heavy when Olivia admitted she used my situation to get Bryan a new client.

"Olivia, enough!" I blurted out after she tried to defend her indefensible action.

"Keep it down," she directed, looking around the café. She lowered her voice and pointed her index finger at me, "You're the one who told me Brunchies was shopping around! You should be happy we're trying to build our business. Doesn't LaToulle make enough money?"

"Ya know, even if that made sense, you should've at least had the audacity to tell me, warn me, anything!"

"What does it matter? You landed them anyway, so why do you care?"

"That's not the point! What if I hadn't? God, Olivia, you never think about anyone but yourself! The whole time I thought you were supporting me, you were only worried about getting Bryan as a client."

"Are you kidding?"

"No, I'm not. Truthfully, you're obsessed with him and will do anything to get him to be with you. You should just be honest about it."

"Oh, kind of like you and Adam?" she shot back.

"Yes, kind of like Adam, who you also didn't warn me would be there. If you were half decent, you'd realize how toxic that guy is, yet you put *his* wants above mine too! You never even told me you gave him my number in the first place. Don't you see why people get annoyed with you?"

"Whose people? Sisi?" She grew more irritated, which only fueled me more. I rarely got angry, but this was too much for me not to go off.

"Yes. And she's right. You haven't even apologized to me yet. You do realize my boss found out about Lola's? You did the same thing to me that you did to Sisi."

"How dare you."

"How dare you! We're over you, your escapades, and your inability to think or care about anyone else but yourself. Sisi's needed you. I've needed you, and you continue to only focus on Olivia."

I guess she ran out of ammo because she huffed, grabbed her bag, and stormed off. "We're not friends anymore!" she shouted over the rows of people dining for lunch.

At the same time, the waiter appeared with our food. In true Olivia fashion, she left me with the bill and the embarrassment of sitting in front of strangers after our fight. At least this would be the last time.

"I'll take it to go," I told the waiter.

After work, I stopped by Lola's. July and August were always the slowest months, so I took this week off to redirect my time toward the new Brunchies account.

"Damn, where did that come from?" Sisi asked after she indulged in my story about lunch with Olivia. We sat at the main bar, which was deserted, each visitor opting to sit on the rooftop instead.

"Years in the making, I suppose. Was I too hard on her?" I double-checked because the whole confronting people thing was new to me.

"Well, it was blunt, but she needed to hear it." She poured herself a beer.

"Ugh, you're right. Should I reach out to—?"

"No. Forget it. She sucks." Sisi cut me off and took a sip. "Kind of like this beer. Yuck!"

I took a sip too. "Yuck, this is gross."

"To Olivia, RIP." Sisi poured some of the beer into the sink behind the bar.

"To Olivia." I mimicked her, and we laughed.

"Come. Let's get your tips from the other night." On our way to the office, I couldn't help but ask about Noah.

"Is he coming back here anytime soon?"

"No! We got everything covered. We actually have a new general manager! Well, in two weeks anyway."

I congratulated her and told her about my weekend—that Noah revealed he was seeing someone.

"What a loser! I knew I didn't like him."

"You don't?" I asked. I couldn't tell by how much she bantered with him.

"Nah, I actually love Noah, but you've always known he's not dating material!" *True!*

"Well, if you thought that was bad, I went home with Adam after."

"Got it out of your system, huh?"

"Sure did. Let's pour some for that too." I poured more of the bad tasting beer into the sink.

"What a week," Sisi conceded.

That it was. But it wasn't over. Step three—talk to Milo.

For Two, Please

———

Since meeting Milo, I never worried if he'd text me back. But it'd been two hours since I asked him to dinner, and I still didn't have a response. I almost convinced myself he was over me when my phone finally pinged.

Milo: Sure.

His colorless response wasn't lost on me, but I was nevertheless reassured that he agreed. We decided to meet at Lola's and walk until we found a place.

Seeing Milo, I realized just how much I valued the comfort of his presence. His genuinity radiated like the warmth of direct sunlight. He was extra tan from his weekend at the beach, and the stubby dark facial hair he grew while away felt sharp when he kissed me.

"I missed you," I said.

"I missed you too." His voice was more mellow than usual. He hugged me. "Ready to go?" He grabbed my hand, and we walked down the street.

"Bye, my dude." Lola's bouncer tapped Milo on his back on our way out. "Take care of her." My heart melted knowing

Milo had formed a bond with my Lola's coworkers. *Seriously, what wasn't there to like?*

The heat outside faded from the day, and the night offered a cooler breeze. We walked to a nearby bar that the Lola's staff frequented. The candlelight reflected from the table onto Milo's smile, his dimple emitting a juvenile charm. My heart warmed more than ever before.

"You're beautiful," he said unequivocally. It was music to any girl's ears, to be with someone you built a connection with who genuinely liked you too. "But we need to talk."

"Wait, I need to talk to you first." I couldn't wait any longer. He looked at me, lowering his glance as if giving me permission to speak. "I like us together. And I've loved my time with you. But I'm scared. I'm scared to be vulnerable and to open myself up to one person, even though you make me feel safe." Milo nodded as the waiter came by to drop off two glasses of wine.

"Your pinot noirs."

"Thank you," I replied and turned back to Milo. He moved his shoulders and jerked his head uncomfortably. He let out a sigh.

"Just because I'm safe doesn't mean you see a future with me," Milo said, nearly confirming what I hoped he wanted.

"Do you see one with me?" I asked, direct and unafraid.

"Look, Kay, I only want you. But I need to know if you feel the same way. I can't do the whole dating around, being uncertain about things. Especially not with you." I knew his words were a result of my negligence during the weekend and lack of commitment thus far.

"So, do you see a future with me?" I pushed him further. Milo paused and took a sip of his wine. A smile slowly emerged on his face.

"Of course I do. I can't stand to think that you wouldn't be mine." When the words left his mouth, a smile emerged on mine too. "I thought about you all weekend," he continued. "How we can build a life here together, support one another. You're smart, you're gorgeous, and… I know it's soon, but shit, Kay. I fucking love you."

Without saying another word, I moved my chair next to his and kissed him.

"Does this mean you'll be my girlfriend?" he asked. I wasn't ready to say I love you, not just yet. But I was ready for this.

"Yes! And that's the last time you have to ask." I committed. No games, no nonsense. I just wanted Milo, the handyman, with a heart of gold who made me laugh, smile, and challenged the way I approached life.

Back at my apartment, we had intimate sex. It wasn't wild or crazy. It was loving and passionate. I let myself be uninhibited, still sexy, but with the sense of knowing this was more than just a moment. This was us. Milo and Kay. And I didn't need anything else.

I woke to find Milo wasn't in bed, but this time I didn't like it. *Where is he?* I almost panicked before I heard clanking noises from my kitchen.

To no avail, Milo woke up early and made me breakfast. Almond flour banana pancakes with 100 percent maple syrup on the side. "Pancakes, eh?" I asked.

"Good morning, girlfriend." He kissed my forehead, his face spotted with flour. I found his keenness for making me happy so sexy. As sexy as the shirt hanging over his shoulder looked as he flipped the last pancake.

"I have to run to work, but you should know that no matter what happens today, you're amazing and can do anything." He placed a fluffy pancake on a plate.

"You didn't have to do all this," I said.

"I wanted to. And you're going to have to get used to me doing nice things for you." He placed a second pancake on my plate. "But, okay, for real, I need to go. My client already called twice." He threw on his shirt, kissed my forehead again, and ran out.

I looked at the plate of pancakes. They looked scrumptious, especially next to my brewed coffee.

Do I deserve this? Yes, Kay. Yes, you do.

Round for the House

—

At LaToulle, Andre greeted me with Samantha news yet again. "She tried calling you, you know."

"Seriously? It's only eight o'clock."

"She's on Euro time, sweetie. Conference room C. I'll tell her you're here." I huffed and jumped on the video call. Samantha joined instantly.

"Kay, how are you?" she asked.

"Good! I'm eager to work on the event debrief for you and Myra today." I tried deflecting from whatever this was really about. My second job? The photos, maybe?

"Great, but that's not why I'm calling." I remained silent, awaiting Samantha's reveal. "The truth is, I thought more about this whole second job thing. I was going to wait until I got back, but... you're getting the promotion." I gasped, totally caught off guard.

"Before you get too excited, this means you need to quit your restaurant gig. We can't ruin our reputation—well, my reputation." *What does she mean, "her reputation"? And who told her about it in the first place?* "Anyway, keep this hush-hush for now. I'll be back Thursday, and we'll discuss your salary, commission, and all that boring stuff." *Not so boring, actually.* "Ah, have to go! I'm getting a call." She hung up abruptly. I collapsed my head on the table. I'd wanted this moment for months. *Why doesn't it feel as good as I expected?*

When I didn't think I could be more overwhelmed, I got a text.

Adam: Thinking of you.

I wanted to throw my phone to avoid Adam and cry at my frustration toward Samantha. But I didn't do either. I recited one of the quotes from my meditation class, *"You're not responsible for your first thought, but you are responsible for your second thought and your first action."* I took a breath and channeled the courageous energy I knew was within me to do what I should have done a long time ago. I blocked Adam.

I spent the next few minutes digesting Samantha's words, "You're getting the promotion," like I was a child anxiously awaiting a piece of candy. "You're getting the promotion," like I would immediately quit Lola's for the sake of Samantha's reputation. "You're getting the promotion," echoed over and over until Andre knocked on the door.

"Can you get yourself up? The VPs need the room."

I noodled on Samantha's words the next couple of days as my colleagues found out about my job at Lola's, otherwise known as "the reason a company-wide email went out." The real kicker? I didn't care. I shed my invisible cloak of shame as the office gossip swirled around me. Instead, I focused on my next steps.

So, when a *Moxy* recruiter set up a call with myself and Tiffany—I took it. And when that went well, and she set up a subsequent in-person interview with Tiffany to discuss a job offer, I unapologetically took that too.

On the day of my interview, I was excited to see Tiffany again in person, only this time without latex shorts on. I wore an ankle-length, Kelly green shimmering skirt with a fitted white tank. My auburn hair was long and wavy over my shoulders, my gold bangles jingling when I moved. It was an outfit for someone who thought she could accomplish anything, and today that was me.

I took a crosstown bus past Central Park South to *Moxy*'s headquarters in Columbus Circle. Their office doors sat adjacent to an international news network, both webbed within a luxury shopping center. Outside Tiffany's office, the receptionist was calm but welcoming.

"You can enter Tiffany's office now," she told me. I stood up and took a deep breath before bypassing her sleek silver desk, covered in bright flowers. The atmosphere was warm and welcoming, a departure from LaToulle's sterile ambiance.

"Kay, how nice it is to see you." Tiffany pushed her laptop to the side, her desk also with flowers and several photos of what I imagined were her family and colleagues.

"It's great to see you again too!"

"Yes, yes, please sit." She gestured her hand to the chair across from her desk. "I know I spent our last call learning all about you, so today, I want to tell you more about me." I nodded in agreement, relieved this wasn't a deeper interview. "I've worked at *Moxy* for more than twenty years. As you know, we're still growing, and fast. Not in the traditional print ads or billboards you're used to, but in commercial advertisement—television, movies, influencers. The senior marketing manager role will broker ad placements across those mediums."

My face lit up. "Wow, that would be a dream role!"

"I saw what you did with Myra's brand, and she raved about you. She also told me you work at that restaurant." *Ah, so it was Myra who said something.* I must have looked shocked because Tiffany coaxed me. "You see, that's the kind of hustle I admire. Some folks don't get that. You know, I usually don't tell this story. But I, too, worked in hospitality for years. I was even a go-go dancer at one point." She looked down at herself. "Trust me, my body was a lot different back then." We both chuckled. "It's what made me promise I'd always treat my staff with the utmost respect, because I know what it's like to have customers and management beat you down, all while you keep a smile on your face."

"Wow, I guess I never realized..."

"Realized what?"

"That Lola's would be seen as a good thing in my career."

"Never be ashamed of a hustle, Kay. It makes you stand out from those who've had things handed to them. Not to say they're not smart, hard workers. But you and I are cut from a different cloth. Big things will come your way, whether here or anywhere else. But you have to own who you are. Don't shy away from it."

"Here?" I asked.

"Yes, of course, we want you for the role, reporting directly to me. The offer is ready for you. I'll email it over, and you take the next couple of days to think about it. But we want you here, so I hope you'll consider."

"Oh, um, yes, of course. Of course, I'll consider."

"Good. Now get out of my office. I've got things to do," she joked before asking her assistant to see me out.

I left the meeting like I won the lottery. The email I got next almost confirmed I had.

Dear Kay,

On behalf of Moxy Media, we'd like to extend you the role of senior marketing manager.

I scrolled past the standard text to unveil the salary and benefits offered, which far exceeded my expectations.

- *$145,000 base salary*
- *Twenty vacation days, three personal days, and five sick days*
- *6 percent 401K Match*
- *Stock options, to accrue year over year*
- *Medical, dental, vision, and HSA account offered*
- *Life insurance*

  And the cherry on top
- *Up to $125,000 commission-based bonus annually*

I texted a photo of the offer to Milo.

Milo: That's my girl.

A Toast

Samantha arrived from vacation more vibrant and tanner than she already was. As if jet lag didn't exist, she whizzed around all morning until the moment I'd been waiting for—to find out my promotion benefits.

"Kay, can you come in here?" she asked from her office. Her voice rattled me, but this time I didn't wish to curl up at home. I took a seat in Samantha's office, gazing out the tall windows behind her desk as she typed the last words of an email. I reminded myself, *No matter the outcome, this city has so much for you. You have so much for you.*

"Congratulations again on your promotion. I'm sure you're ready to hear about your new salary, so let's not waste time." I widened my eyes and smiled a forced look of gratitude, despite the layer of anxiety beneath my surface. I imagined I'd get into the six-figure range with a client lead role, but truthfully, I had zero evidence to support this theory and feared potential disappointment.

"Starting September first, you will have a 15 percent raise." I did the mental math to calculate my new salary. I currently make $65,000, so this brought me to just under $75,000.

Seventy-five thousand! Was this a joke? I just brought us in a three-quarters of a million-dollar account.

"You're also getting a bonus from now on. Five thousand annually if you hit your targets, which we'll set for you. We don't typically add this much, but you brought in a lot of revenue this year!" She raised her voice with excitement, as if the offer was abundant and I should be jubilant. "This has it all in writing." She handed me a folder. "Congratulations again."

I took the folder, a symbol of my feared disappointment coming to fruition. But it wasn't so bad. Not with my offer from *Moxy* on the table.

"Oh, and please. Keep this tight-lipped for a few more hours. I plan to announce promotions over drinks tonight. I'm taking everyone out!" I could have told Samantha about my competing job offer, but I decided to wait. I worked hard for my promotion. So, if I couldn't enjoy the satisfaction of a higher salary at LaToulle, I'd at least relish in the announcement of my new job title to colleagues.

—

In a private room at an upscale restaurant in midtown, about twenty-five LaToulle employees sat around a long dinner table. Samantha tapped her glass to capture our attention. "It takes a special team to carry an office without the owner around, so tonight is for you!" We cheers'd our champagne flutes. "I know you're all hungry, so let's order some food before we get into the good news."

Finally, I saw through Samantha, her walls more transparent now. She used her reputation and smart staff to be selfishly frivolous. The worst part, we didn't get fair compensation for any of it.

"All right! Team!" After we ordered, Samantha captured our attention again. "I have a few announcements to make, all too fabulous not to share at a fabulous restaurant, drinking fabulous champagne." She looked at her flute. "This champagne is a client, by the way, so if you haven't taken a photo and tagged them online, please do." Right away, some of my colleagues took out their phones to do so. "Not right now! Wait until I'm done speaking!" Those same colleagues quickly put their phones down.

"Kay," she continued, and my ears perked up. "... she has been promoted to client lead. She'll be running campaigns and branding for our major accounts while overseeing some smaller accounts." I surveyed the room for my team's response. A lot of nodding, like they expected this. "You've brought in a great deal of work this year with the vision to carry it through, which deserves big recognition," Samantha said. *Just not a big raise.*

Samantha then acknowledged our assistant vice president, who'd been promoted to vice president. And then shared news neither myself nor my coworkers expected.

"And last but not least, Natasha has also been promoted." When I looked around this time, my coworkers seemed shocked, their eyes open or jaws dropped. "Natasha has executed high caliber events recently. She's client focused and detailed oriented, and given we have a growing client list, there's a need for us to host our own events instead of outsourcing to vendors. So, Natasha, you have a newly created title of event manager."

I looked at Natasha, who looked back at me, neither of us as cheery as you'd expect after hearing your promotion announced. Then, Natasha rolled her eyes, which made me giggle. All the time we'd spent worrying about one another's success seemed to be for nothing.

"Let's give a hand to your newly promoted coworkers! Cheers!" My colleagues clapped for us again.

"Look at you, working your way up," Andre said after we ate. "You know, you got that promotion pretty quick. I've been here forever, but I'll always just be Samantha's right-hand man." *Was he signaling something?*

"Do you like your role?" I asked.

"Oh, love it! You know Samantha loves me, gives me all her samples and bonuses during the year. I'm lucky to work for her, even if she emails me all hours of the night and has me managing her personal calendar. But, you know, the grass isn't always greener."

No, it isn't. But who wants to stay around for free samples, small bonuses, and a needy manager when you can have a higher salary, a chunky bonus, and a boss who respects you? Andre's reality was my biggest work fear realized.

After Samantha paid the bill and said her goodbyes, most people trickled out behind her with the exception of a few of us who lingered behind.

"Didn't I tell you you'd get the promotion?" Natasha lightly elbowed my arm.

"Yeah, yeah." I waved my hand to dismiss her. "But look at you! Event manager, huh?"

"Honestly, I'm not good at the creative stuff, so it's a huge relief not to have to do it anymore. I didn't want to admit it before, but Kay, it's clear to everyone—you're amazing at what you do."

"You think so?" I asked bashfully. Natasha looked at me like, *C'mon.*

"You don't know that by now? You literally just got a promotion." *She had a point.* "Hopefully, it means we work alongside each other instead of against one another," she continued.

"Well, I have some news about that. I'm actually leaving LaToulle." I wanted to tell Natasha first.

"*What*? Does anyone know?"

"Shh," I motioned my index finger over my lips. "No! I'm telling Samantha tomorrow, and I'm sure it will be around the office as fast as the news about my second job was." Natasha laughed.

"So, I'm the first to know? Wow, we've really come full circle," she said.

"Seriously," I let out a light laugh and took a sip of my champagne.

"Wait, also, no one cares about your second job. Well, maybe no one besides Samantha."

"Huh?" I asked, puzzled.

"Yeah, she brought it up at a meeting today. Asked that we let her know if we have other things going on outside of work. Kind of weird, honestly."

I rolled my eyes, thankful I'd be leaving LaToulle's and not have to worry about this any longer.

"Actually," Natasha continued, "since you're leaving and all, I guess I can tell you. Andre showed me a separate email Myra sent Samantha. She went hard on her but praised you. I didn't want to say anything because Andre told me not to, but I promise you I didn't tell Samantha about Lola's—Myra did."

"In the email?"

"Yeah, it was in her rave about how hard you work. It was all positive! But it probably caught Samantha by surprise. Who knows why, she pays us nothing and… Well, whatever, working at a restaurant is pretty cool if you ask me."

I nodded, hoping there'd be no more sneaking through emails or hiding my truth at *Moxy*. "Thanks for letting me know." I tapped my glass against hers.

"Anytime. Just don't forget about me when you leave here."
She smiled before grabbing her coat to leave.

From enemies to frenemies to, dare I say, friends, Natasha and I had come a long way from our first days at LaToulle, and it was another reason to be thankful tonight.

Cheers

The next morning, I accepted Tiffany's offer and was ready to deny Samantha's. I knocked on her office door—no help from Andre, no meeting scheduled.

"Have a minute? There's something I need to talk to you about." Without a chance to sit down, Samantha started.

"Oh, is it about the restaurant? I'll need you dedicated here more. No more waitressing or whatever you do. That should be fine considering your raise, right?" I closed the door and calmly took a seat.

"Thank you, Samantha, but that's not what I want to talk about."

"Oh, okay. What?"

"I got a job offer with Moxy Media as their senior marketing manager, and I'm going to take it. Their compensation offer is more than double my new offer here, and it's a job I'm really excited about." I was pragmatic, with no short breaths or sweaty palms to deter me. "I start in mid-August, so I'll take the next two weeks to finish out my role here."

Samantha pulled her head back in disbelief. "Wow, well, okay. You said double the pay?"

"Yes," I responded.

"Well, we can't do that. Geez, that's a lot." Samantha let out a dramatic breath and placed her hands on her desk. "Well, okay, wrap up your work and offload it to Natasha for me. Andre will help you with offboarding." Without a congratulations or compliment from Samantha, I said okay, and left her office.

After work, I stopped at Lola's to officially quit. Only when I went to the office, there was no Sisi. Instead of her blonde highlights, I saw messy blonde hair. It was Noah.

"Oh, hey there," he said. My heart raced for a moment before I reminded myself I didn't need to be nervous. He was seeing someone, and I was in a new, happy relationship. We weren't anything more or less.

"Hey, Noah. What are you doing here?"

"I needed to stop by to get something from Si, but I'm just on my way out. Are you working today?"

"No, I'm not working here anymore." Part of me wanted to brag about my new job to show off. But I didn't. There was no need to prove anything to him. "I need to find Sisi, so I'll catch you later," I said.

"Yeah, all right. I'm just about to leave too. Nice to see you." He smiled, and I went upstairs. I spent a split moment fantasizing about what could have been with him. Then, I cut the thought off. *What was the point?*

Upstairs, Sisi had just walked in from a coffee run. "Do you see the way they wrote my name? It's S-I-S-I, not C-E-C-E. Ugh!" I laughed before telling her about my new job offer.

"Well, that's just great, Kay! This way, I don't have to fire you!"

"What? Fired?"

"Kidding! I'll miss you working here, but your career trumps any of my feelings. I couldn't be more proud of you!"

"Thank you, Si! Does this mean I get a hug?

"Um, no. But it does mean I don't have to worry about your schedule anymore."

"Well, lucky you!"

I left to get ready for my date night with Milo. He wanted to take me out to celebrate and sent me the coordinates for where to meet. I wasn't sure why he didn't just send me the restaurant name. That was until I arrived. The coordinates led me to our first date spot.

Inside, Milo sat at the same loveseat by the window. His freshly cut hair brought out his hazelnut eyes and tan, further illuminated by the dim light above us.

"How are you, babe?" I never thought I'd enjoy someone calling me *babe,* but with him, it felt so good.

"I'm great! Because guess what?"

"What?"

"I just quit Lola's!"

"Oh yeah, until when? Sisi will probably call you next week for help."

I laughed. "True, but she has a bigger staff now, so I think I'm actually done for good."

"I say you'll miss that place and be back in a few months," Milo rebutted. I smirked, knowing he may be right.

"Okay, but guess what else?"

"What?" he asked, his mouth open.

"I put in my two weeks with LaToulle!"

"That's my girl!"

Over dinner, we talked about my new role and final conversation with Samantha. Milo couldn't be happier for me and ordered a flourless chocolate cake and a bottle of red wine to celebrate.

"Do you remember our first date here?" Milo asked.

"Of course! I remembered how cute I thought you were, even though you talked a lot." I laughed and took a bite of warm cake.

Always taking well to my humor, Milo laughed too. "Well, I've been thinking a lot. I know we've only been official for, like, forty-eight hours, but it's been months since we met, and I love being with you so much."

"You too!" I interjected, out of excitement and because it was true.

"Okay, this is kind of cheesy to say, but you're like the girl of my dreams. And if I was distant on my trip, I'm sorry. I just noticed we were falling into a routine, and I don't want you to get bored, and I don't want to mess this up." Poor Milo didn't think of what I could have been up to that same weekend. But there was no point in rehashing—it was officially water under the bridge. "I want to be with you. Really be with you. I can see myself spending my life with you."

Was he about to propose? Part of me was humbled and smitten by his words, and another part felt nervous and terrified that I would have to say "no." I liked him but wasn't ready for this!

"Anyway," he continued, "we have to make a promise to each other. To always keep our relationship fresh. I don't ever want you to get bored. Because, well, I love you, Kay. And I really want each day to feel like our first together."

Overcome with a wave of relief, I said what was in my heart. "I love you, too, Milo." Because I did. I loved how he cared for me. I loved our budding partnership. And I loved that he thought to bring us to the place our spark first ignited. We kissed over the loveseat.

"And, okay... there's one more thing. Not to steal from *our* shine, but I have something to show you," I said

"*Your* shine *is* our shine, babe. Show me."

I pulled from my purse a printed copy of an article Lilly had drafted. It was about my new role at Moxy Media. I folded the headline, only to reveal the cover photo—a Polaroid of me holding a bucket of Brunchies at the Lola's party.

"Woah! You look awesome. Was that the event I missed?" I nodded and lifted the folded part of the paper. The headline read, "...with a splash of Kay."

"Hey! That was my line!" Milo said.

"I know! I loved when you said it, so I nudged the idea to Lilly, who also loved it. The entire article is about how I helped morph Brunchies to become the 'fall trend to look out for.' Look, she writes here, '*Moxy*'s newest member, Kay Mitchell, knows what you'll be sipping before you do.'"

"Ha, that's great. I want to read the whole thing." Which he did right away. "We need to frame this in your apartment. Has Myra seen it?"

"Yes! She loves it and loves that I'm working with *Moxy*. She's dropping LaToulle and will be my first client. Tiffany wants to feature Brunchies in a new teen drama on Netflix!"

"I seriously couldn't be more proud of you," Milo said and kissed me again. *I couldn't be more proud of me either.*

That night, tipsy and on a date night high, we had slow, passionate sex in my apartment. We lay together, talking for an hour until Milo nodded off. I was just about to fall asleep, too, when my phone pinged. *Who could this be?*

> **Noah:** Great to see you earlier. Maybe we
> should talk.

I almost replied but decided not to. It would mean defying our guilt for selfish pleasure that likely wouldn't amount to anything anyway. We would fade, but our actions wouldn't. So, in the end, there was no point. I didn't explore that potential next chapter, even if short-lived. I figured it best to be left with thoughts of Noah and me than consequences.

—

I laid awake at six-thirty the next morning, my thoughts picking up where I left them before bed. I fantasized about Noah. I replayed his smile and our kiss again in my mind. Until Milo's snore laid right into me. A clear reminder I wasn't living that fantasy and I wasn't alone. I shook off the thoughts and turned toward him.

He was awake now, smiling his most adorable, warm smile. "Te amo," he said, moving my hair out of my face and behind my ear. I moved closer so we could embrace. My other thoughts vanished when I remembered, *this is home.*

Acknowledgments

Thank you to all those who provided me with encouragement that helped carry me through this effort. A special thank you to Michael Barnhart, Kathleen Benoit, Kaitlyn Benoit, Sabrina Blackburn, Aly Denegri, Sharon Gardiner, Rachel Fohrman, Janet Meyer, Rachel Pacheco, Megan Pickarski, Curtis Stewart, Hillary Taubman, Jessy Tolkan, Catherine Zagorski, and Katie Zigelman for providing your time or financial support to make this happen.

Author's Note

Many of you have followed me on this journey, but to those who haven't, I finally made one of my dreams to be a fiction author come true!

Growing up, I clung to fun, uplifting stories about women like they were my own. I fell in love with comedy-dramas like *Sex and the City* and engaging books like *City of Girls*. I valued their combination of relatability with entertainment and escapism.

For years, I've had a deep desire to write a story that provided the same experience for others. And, as any artist knows, when your creative match is sparked, it's pretty difficult to put out. It is my hope that in reading this book, you will find a little bit of yourself in the main character, Kay Mitchell. Throughout the pages, I want you to relate to her circumstances and learn alongside her path of self-discovery the same way you may have with other characters from your favorite TV shows or books. And equally important, I want you to have a good time reading! ... *with a splash of Kay* is intended to be fun and lighthearted. It may even make you laugh.